BLACK LIGHT: WANTED

MAREN SMITH

Black Light: Wanted
by Maren Smith

Published by Black Collar Press
Don't miss a release! Sign-up for our newsletter here!

EBook ISBN: **978-1-947559-50-9**
Print ISBN: **978-1-947559-51-6**

Cover Art by Eris Adderly, http://erisadderly.com/

BLURB

He had her the longest... he hurt her the most...

Anna "Pony" Mitchell should be dead. Abandoned by her
Menagerie sisters and shot by the only man she's ever loved,
now the hospital has declared her "unfit." She has thirty days
to prove them wrong or spend the rest of her life hospitalized.

He lost his leg, his job... and almost his life.

Marcus Hawke knows he's not much good to anyone
anymore, but when an old friend calls in a favor, he doesn't
say no. It's been years since he's deprogrammed anyone this
badly wounded, but for every inch of progress she gains, he
soon realizes he's got bigger problems. It doesn't matter what
lies he tells himself, she isn't just a job anymore.

He wants her...

But after all she's been through, she deserves better than
what a half-man can give.

She wants him...

But after all he's been through, he's made it clear he'll never be her dom.

PROLOGUE

Anna/Pony

*P*ony lay on her side in the narrow hospital bed and stared unblinking at the wall. Master Ethen was dead. He'd shot her in the head. The Menagerie he'd wanted so much was disbanded. Even Puppy had abandoned her, and now he was dead.

If only she were dead too.

For four years, she'd given herself to Master in every way a good slave could. His every whim had been her gospel. She'd dressed in the clothes he'd selected, worked the jobs he'd chosen, driven the car he'd allowed her to buy, cooked and eaten only his most favorite things. She'd given him everything—from every scrap of property she'd owned since before she met him, to her paychecks. She'd thought what he'd wanted her to think. Spoken the opinions he'd wanted her to have. Shared her body with him, whenever, wherever, and however he'd desired it.

Not once had she ever said no. Not when he was in a mood to hurt and debase her.

Not even when he was in a mood to watch her with other men.

She had been his. Heart, mind, body, and soul. She had never wanted anyone else. Only him.

Always him.

And he'd shot her in the head.

Pony closed her eyes, telling herself that the tears that kept burning her eyes were because her head hurt so badly. It wasn't.

He hadn't wanted her. She'd been his, the first slave he'd taken in as part of his Menagerie, gifted with the title of lead submissive and tasked with keeping the others in line. She'd tried. Oh, how she'd tried. Even after Piggy and Kitty ran away and he'd been sent to jail, she'd stayed and done her best to keep the rebelling Puppy obedient to his wishes. But it hadn't mattered. He'd wanted Puppy, Piggy, Kitty… everyone —anyone. He just hadn't wanted her.

Curling in around herself, Pony made herself as small as the hospital bed would allow. The IV in her arm was pumping fluids into her system. She had bruises from the back of both hands to her elbows where the IV had blown out her veins. If it happened again, they said, they'd have no choice but to try the veins in her feet. She was too malnourished, they said, and she knew she was thin. She could see the proof of it every time she looked in the mirror and in the heavy loss of long blonde strands caught in the drain when she showered. There wasn't a lot she could do about it, though. When Master Ethen said no food, she didn't eat. It was just that simple and just that hard, especially since most of her punishments these days were because of Puppy.

Disobedient, traitorous Puppy, whose mother had shot Master after he'd shot Pony. In the head. While she'd been running to pack her things so she could at last, now that he'd finally been released from prison, go back home with him.

Things were supposed to be back to normal now, but they would never be normal again. So, what did it matter how thin she was or how many meals she'd missed? In the last year, she'd missed a lot of meals, but not once had she ever cheated on him. Lately, she'd even come to kind of like the hollow-feeling pinch in her stomach. Regardless of what Puppy was doing—running around with that man who wasn't their Master—at least *she* was being obedient.

She was being good.

She was being worth his time and attention.

And he'd shot her at just the right distance, with just the right caliber of bullet, that it had skimmed the back of her skull rather than penetrating the bone. She'd felt the impact like a sledgehammer. It hadn't just knocked her down, it had knocked her out cold. She didn't remember hitting the floor. She only remembered coming to in the ambulance with her face stiff and sticky with blood and the mother of all headaches pounding at her temples and behind her eyes.

"You should buy a lottery ticket," said the doctor who'd examined her once she reached the hospital. "This is a one-in-a-million outcome for a headshot. I don't know why it didn't kill you."

She'd sat there, numb while the doctor stapled the gash in the back of her scalp back together and the detective handling her 'case' filled in the massive blank where her memory showed her only blackness instead of what had actually happened. Reassuring her yet again that she was safe now that her attacker was dead, the detective had then asked her questions.

She hadn't answered them. She'd barely heard them. Her Master was dead.

The man she had loved with all the diligence and obedience that her too-thin body possessed had been killed.

Murdered.

After he'd shot her. In the head. Because he'd wanted to kill her more than he'd wanted to keep her with him.

She stared at the wall directly in front of her, not moving, only blinking even when she heard the door to her room open. Unlike the nurses with their squeaky shoes, the footsteps that entered behind her were slow and almost silent as they approached the bed. After a moment, a chair was drawn up to her beside. It creaked under the weight of whoever sat.

"Hello, Anna," said the voice of a man she didn't recognize.

Unmoving, Pony kept her gaze fixed on the wall. She didn't greet him back.

"My name is Marcus Hawke. I'm a friend of Spencer's. I've been asked to help you."

It took her a moment to process who he meant. She only knew one Spencer, and he was the manager of the east coast branch of Black Light, one of the best BDSM-oriented clubs in the States. Master had hated the man, a sentiment Spencer had returned in spades. He'd been nothing but cold toward them for almost as long as they'd been going to Black Light, right up until he'd banned them from coming back. Because he was jealous of him, Master had said. Master was the better Dom and the pathetic club manager couldn't stop lusting after Master's menagerie girls.

If he were alive, Master would tell her neither Spencer, nor his friends, were worth their time.

Her jaw clenched and her stare hardened as she stared fixedly at the wall.

"Okay." The chair creaked as the man, Marcus, got up. Dragging the chair behind him, he rounded the foot of the bed. Out of the periphery of her vision, she noted him via the most abstract details—the snug fit of his worn jeans, the glint of silver off his rodeo belt buckle, the hug of his white polo shirt, and the bulge of his muscular forearms as he came around the end of the bed with a slight limp to his step and set the padded chair down directly in front of her.

Clean shaven, he looked to be in his mid-forties. His skin was tan and weathered from years in the sun. His eyes were stone gray, she noted, fighting not to look at him directly but to keep her glare fixed on the wall. His hair was brown and just long enough to tie back into a ponytail.

Giving the crease at the thighs of his jeans a tug, he favored his right leg as he sat back down. Elbows on knees and big hands folded together, he brought himself down to her level, physically blocking her stubborn view so she had no choice but to look at him.

Except she did have a choice, and she refused. She glared at his ear instead and did her best not to satisfy his invasion of her privacy with even the smallest reaction.

"Like I said," he continued mildly. "My name is Marcus Hawke, and I was asked to take your case."

She already had a detective. She didn't need another one.

"I know you've been through a lot," he said. "Obviously, you'd rather not talk to me, but I'm here anyway. So, unless you tell me to go fuck myself, then I'll do the talking and you can do all the listening. Agreed?"

Her jaw clenched, but Pony said nothing.

"I'll take that as consent. Okay, let's do this." Tipping his head, Marcus put his face directly into her staring path. Refusing to give him the satisfaction of making her acknowledge him, she glared at him directly now. "Your name is Anna Mitchell."

She could see it in his dark, knowing eyes. He was waiting to see if she would protest his use of it.

"Or I could call you Pony, if you prefer." He waited again,

and only after her lengthy silence added, "No? Well, Anna it is, then."

Master Ethen he was not, not even close.

"Your life has gone through a hell of an upheaval," Marcus noted, seeming not the slightest bit bothered by her disrespectful stare. "Unfortunately, if I'm involved, then the upheavals aren't yet over."

He shifted in his chair far enough to reach into his back jeans pocket and pull out a thin packet of folded papers. He held them up for her to see.

"This," he said, making himself comfortable again, "is a temporary court order granting me legal guardianship over one Miss Anna Mitchell until such a time as your competency can be proven with relative satisfaction. We've an uphill battle ahead of us. The doctors here are advocating for you to be hospitalized. It's their opinion that you aren't mentally sound and I'll tell you, this vaguely hostile silent treatment you've got going isn't helping anyone."

Her chest was so tight she couldn't feel herself breathing. He couldn't be serious. She wanted to snatch the papers from his hand, but her muscles were locked up tight and her arms refused to move.

"Still nothing to say?" he asked, giving her every opportunity to protest.

Stubbornness and fury rising hot and fast to fill up every grieving corner of her being, she shook from the effort it took to hold it silently in.

"All right then, let's continue. You're five-foot-six and you weigh eighty-seven pounds. You were living in a house with plentiful access to healthy food, so you're going to need to come up with an explanation for why you're this malnourished and dehydrated if you don't want the courts to side with your doctors. Unfortunately, your medical charts now include the diagnosis 'anorexia nervosa.' Fortunately, eating disorders, while considered mental illnesses, don't usually lead to hospitalization. Which takes us right back to your next 'unfortunately,' because we both know that's not what's going on here, don't we?"

She swallowed hard, locking her jaw.

"You've got marks all over your body," he continued evenly, his returning stare steady and neutral, despite the accusation in his words. "Old, new, infected and scarring. They've chalked it down to self-harm and it's obvious it's been going on for a while. I don't for a second doubt that you have punished yourself, but I think I also know where the order to do it came from. Am I wrong?"

"Don't talk about him," Pony warned, breaking her silence for the first time and before she could stop herself.

"He's dead," Marcus said evenly.

"Murdered," she spat.

"I'm very sorry for your loss."

She caught her breath, locking herself in position in bed before every wildly reacting nerve in her body threw her upright so she could scream in his face—*You are not! Nobody is! I loved him!*

Something she would continue to do right up until she died, even though he'd shot her in the head.

In a hot rush, her anger abandoned her, leaving her bereft in that stupid hospital bed with nothing but the burn of tears filling up the back of her throat until it reached her eyes. She blinked furiously.

"You must have loved him very much," Marcus said softly. None of the sympathy she could hear in his voice reached his eyes.

Her breath hitched, catching in her throat as she fought not to cry. "You don't know anything about me."

"I know more than you think," he corrected. "What I don't, you'll have plenty of time to tell me on your own. I've already talked to the nurses. They're bringing your clothes and discharge papers. As soon as you're dressed, we'll leave here together."

"I'm not going anywhere with you," she rasped, the sting of tears growing stronger.

He held up the packet of papers for her to see the court seal on the front. "Yes, Anna, you are. For the next thirty days, I am your legal guardian and don't for a second think this is my first rodeo."

Her gaze dropped to his belt buckle before she could stop herself.

"Not that kind of rodeo." A corner of his mouth curled. "I'm retired now. Before that, I spent eighteen years as a bounty hunter. The last thirteen of those, I spent as a bounty hunter who specialized in deprograming what some people would call mind control—cult members, victims of long-term abuse and/or violent hostage or kidnapping situations. Stockholm Syndrome. That sort of thing."

"I am not a victim," she spat. "I don't have Stockholm's!"

He studied her, but didn't argue. "What makes me uniquely qualified for your case, and the reason Spencer called me is because I have twenty-two years' experience as a Dom. My taste runs toward extreme service submissives, what some would call slaves. I have trained—or programmed—every submissive I've taken. I also have some experience in de-programming submissives who have come from, let's say, the care of inexperienced or abusive so-called masters."

Her anger flared even hotter. Her voice shook now every bit as much as the rest of her. "Master was *not* so-called. You didn't know him! You have no right to talk about him like that! You have no right to talk about him at all! If you think for one second I'm going anywhere with you…"

"Over the course of the next thirty days, we are going to talk about a lot of things that are going to make you very uncomfortable." He waved the packet of papers. "And yes, you are coming with me—"

"Never!"

"—if I have to carry you out of here over my shoulder like a sack of potatoes," he concluded. "This is happening, whether you want it to or not. The only thing you have a choice in is whether you want to cooperate and help me get you the best possible outcome at your competency hearing thirty days from now, or if you want to be difficult, in which case, you are going to find your ability to make your own decisions hampered for quite a long time."

Her jaw dropped. "You can't."

"Read it." He handed her the packet of court documents.

Snatching them from his hand, she promptly ripped them into pieces and threw them back in his face.

"That was a copy," he said mildly. "I've already had it filed with the hospital and my local police department, just in case you decide you want to go that route."

"Get out," she hissed. "I'm not going anywhere with you. Puppy!" she bellowed toward the door.

"Cynthia has her own healing to do. Her Dom took her home, pretty much like I'm about to do with you."

Heart beating hard behind her ribs, she shook her head. "You're not my Dom."

Something she couldn't quite read flittered through his dark eyes, there and gone before she could figure it out. "No, I'm not. I'm nothing like he was, something you should be very grateful for. I'm actually going to treat you with respect. Or at least, I'm going to try to for as long as your behavior allows it."

"And if it doesn't?" she returned. "What are you going to do then, shoot me in the head?"

Been there. Done that. She had the staples in her head to prove it.

His eyes narrowed slightly, considering his next move. She didn't give him the chance.

"I'm not going anywhere with you," she said, rolling over and putting her back to him. "Go away. My head hurts."

She lay down on her right side now, arms tightly folded across her stomach and her legs drawn up. She closed her eyes against the pinch of pain that accompanied her soft contact with the pillow. The staples beneath the gauzy bandage that covered her wound pulled, bringing on another wave of stinging tears that she was determined not to cry.

Because she was Pony—tall, regal, beautiful and aloof.

The first in Master's Menagerie. Foremost in his heart and his home. The one he'd said he would love forever and yet in reality the one he'd preferred the least.

The one he didn't care that he still had if he couldn't also have the others.

The useless one. The worthless one.

The one he'd tried to kill.

Things would have been so much better for everyone if only he'd succeeded.

CHAPTER 1

Marcus

He never should have squatted down in front of Pony's friend, Cynthia, out in the waiting room. Yes, she'd needed to hear that she'd done well in her attempts to take care of Pony. And yes, she'd absolutely needed to hear that she was now free from that incredibly toxic bond, but his lower leg prosthetic hurt at the best of times and it was killing him now. Phantom leg pain, they called it. It had been three years and it hadn't gone away yet, he knew he was stuck with it.

Suck it up, buttercup. Pain means you're still alive.

Yay, him. He shifted his leg, easing the angle of his knee to take some of the pressure off his stump, and waited.

Pony lay with her back to him, her small shoulders way too thin and the edges of what he could see of her cheek and jaw too sharp. Cynthia, the girl Spencer had called Puppy, was bony, but Pony... she was positively skeletal. At first glance, she was the worst case he'd yet tackled, physically. Mentally, he didn't like what he'd thus far seen, but it would be days yet before he was comfortable enough to solidify what he'd assessed—that she was stubborn, angry... hurt. Layers and layers and layers of fiercely buried hurt lay deep in the woman before him, swallowed back the way a dutiful slave submissive would do if he or she didn't know how—or weren't allowed—to voice their needs.

It had been a long time since his last case, but if he was successful at nothing else, he was determined that *that* would be one of the first things he helped her change.

"Good morning," announced a very young woman in nursing scrubs. Too young to have graduated with a masters' in nursing, the assistant strolled cheerfully up to Pony's bedside. When no answering hail was forthcoming, she paused to peer at Pony more closely. "Are we sleeping? Her eyes were closed."

"More like sulking," Marcus corrected.

Pony curled in that much tighter around herself, but she didn't argue. Eventually, he would get her to a point where she felt safe enough that she could. In the meantime, Marcus hunkered down in his chair and did his best to hold onto his own spiking temper as the nursing assistant peeled back Pony's blankets and he took in the rest of Pony's very poor condition. Ethen O'Dowell was no master; he was a criminal and death by bullet had been far too kind. Apart from the clenching of his fist, Marcus didn't move as he counted down the ladder of bumps that was her spine, poking through the gaps in her loosely tied hospital gown.

Noticing the direction of his darkening stare, the assistant quickly adjusted Pony's gown to cover her better. "There, we wouldn't want you to get chilled now," she said, eyeing him uncertainly, but talking to Pony. "Can you sit up for me?"

She didn't move.

"Sit up," Marcus calmly ordered, letting his inner dom inflect every nuance of that command.

Pony responded. Grudgingly, she uncurled and pushed herself up until she was sitting on the edge of the bed. The thinnest damn legs he'd ever seen dangled over the mattress's edge and pinpricks of blood dotted her white pillow where she'd been lying.

"We'll have to change your bandage," the assistant said, bending around to peer at the far side of her head. He couldn't see how much blood was seeping through her bandage, but he could see how much of her head had been shaved. He had to force himself to relax his clenched fists.

"Don't bother," Pony told her. "I'm fine."

The younger woman laughed. "Oh, it's no bother. I'm happy to do it. If I were in your place, I wouldn't want to go out in public with a bloody—"

"I said"—Pony raised her head, instantly abandoned all hints of her former apathy in favor of aggression—"I'm fine."

The assistant lost her smile. Marcus almost found his. There she was—the backbone of the fighter inside of Pony's damaged soul, the one who'd been strong enough to survive her dom's abuse.

"Behave," he ordered, shifting Pony's aggression from the nurse to himself.

Make me flashed through her narrowing blue eyes before just as quickly vanishing as her face shuttered against him. She dropped her gaze to her knees, hiding from him the only way she could, but too late. He'd already seen it and every dominant fiber of his being had just come snapping awake. The start was so vibrant he could physically feel the tingling sting in his skin.

Oblivious to the silent exchange, the nurse rallied her cheerfulness and tried again to get on Pony's good side. "I brought your clothes."

Through the clear plastic bag she set on the bed by Pony's hip, Marcus took note of the dark reddish-brown blood stains on what looked like a white blouse and dark blue business skirt.

"You'll want to change as soon as you get home, of course," said the CNA, "but at least you won't be leaving here in paper scrubs."

He'd need to get her clothes. According to the paperwork he'd been given, filled out in part by the Black Light lawyer who had been hired to help keep her out of state custody, and her friend Cynthia, Pony had very little in the way of personal possessions—just the work outfits for a job she had apparently lost months ago and her harness.

The torso harness that had chafed her ribs and back until her skin opened into sores was now part of the evidence the hospital intended to use against her. And, she wouldn't need work clothes, at least not for a while. In fact, everything from her time with Ethen O'Dowell, Marcus decided, was about to get left behind. If he only had thirty days to help her prove she could take care of herself, then he wasn't going to spend it dealing with the complications that would surely arise by giving her tangible 'master reminders' to hold onto.

A clean break, that's what she needed and that's what he would give her.

Turning to him, the assistant said, "You'll have to step outside now, please."

And give her a chance to either bolt or lash out at the unsuspecting nurse's aide?

"Not a chance," Marcus replied. Having already seen hints of temper in Pony, he wasn't about to go anywhere. Then it occurred to him... not only was he in the civilian world, but he was in the vanilla civilian world. A hospital, a place full to the brim with mandatory reporters who wouldn't understand or care that his rules were geared toward Pony and the world she'd been living in for so long that she could no longer function anywhere else. He would need to make concessions.

"Fine." He stood up, catching himself mid limp as his sore leg protested being too long in its prothesis. Steadying himself, he turned his back, folded his arms across his chest, and did his best not to sound disgruntled about having to bend to the will of the twenty-year-old behind him. "This is as close as you're going to get to me leaving. Now, get her changed or I'll walk her out of the here as she is."

"Um... I just... I don't think..."

He could all but hear the young assistant tapping her fingers in indecision. He really did roll his eyes now. He didn't have time for this. "I'm her legal guardian and I am backed by a court order. I'm not leaving this room without her. Get her dressed. Now."

He turned his head far enough to pin the young woman with a look that had rarely failed to make any of his past submissives jump to obey. His disapproving frown was utterly wasted on the assistant, but not Pony. She stared back at him, her body stiff and her hands clenched in tight fists on her thighs. That serene and unreadable mask she'd tried to don had slipped, laying bare the wistful sadness underneath. The rise and fall of her small breasts had quickened. The white and blue fabric of the hospital gown wasn't thick enough to hide the fact that her nipples had stiffened into peaks.

For all that she was hurt and angry, she was also still a submissive and her body yearned to be taken under a competent dom's command.

"Get out of bed," he told her, more than capable of fulfilling that need. "Get dressed. We're leaving."

That glisten in her eyes became downright watery, and her bottom lip quivered. "I don't want to go with you."

The trickle of that first tear spilling over her lashes to roll unhindered down her too-thin face sparked an unexpected heat in the pit of his belly. Not now, he told him, but his cock stirred against his will. Of all the inappropriate times to get a fucking woody, but he couldn't help it any more than, apparently, she could stop herself from crying. She scrubbed the errant tear away as if embarrassed, but another slipped free and the equally inappropriate urge to taste it on her cheek made his mouth water. Once upon a time, back before his accident and before he'd retired, when he'd still had a submissive of his own, tears used to be his aphrodisiac.

He faced forward again, killing the inappropriate hunger growing inside him under a heavy roll of irritation. "Take the IV out of her and put her goddamn clothes on. I won't repeat myself again."

Two steps was all it took to carry him, despite his gut instincts and earlier objections, out of the room. He stood sentry with the door cracked at his back so he could hear it if Pony's earlier aggression resurged, but the only thing he heard was the aide's nervously whispered, "Should I call someone?"

From Pony, he never heard so much as a sniffle. A few minutes later, the door at his back swung into the room and the young assistant backed out.

"I'll check with her nurse to see where she is in the discharge process."

"Tell her she has fifteen minutes and then we're leaving. We've a long drive and a long day ahead of us, and I'd just as soon get started."

She walked away, glancing back at him over her shoulder. Once upon a time, he'd have gazed back at her with a dominant's assessing eye and a mind tuned toward what kind of kinky play he might be able to coax out of her.

A spanking, the lecherous half of his brain decided. She was young, not yet grown out of her little girl mindset. He was willing to bet he was just 'Daddy' enough to convince her that a trip across his knee was exactly what she needed.

His good knee, preferably.

Which was all it took to kill that half-hearted fantasy. No submissive wanted a broken half-man for a dom.

He turned on his prosthetic and went back inside, to the empty chair waiting by Pony's hospital bed. She sat exactly as he'd left her, back stiff as a broom handle, her masked gaze staring straight at the wall ahead of her. The chair was on the opposite side of the bed behind her. She did not acknowledge him when he came in, batting not so much as an eyelash as he eased into the chair to study her back.

What had it been, three years since he'd last done this? What a disaster that had turned out to be. The client in that case had been a man, trapped inside a cult, in fear of his life and desperate to get his family out. He'd called his parents. His parents had hired him. He'd gone in with a county sheriff at his back, and what should have been a peaceful extraction had turned into a gunfight. The bullet that had shattered both his tibia and fibula never should have claimed his leg, but for the tiny shred of cloth from his pants that got left in the wound after surgery. The resulting infection had hit so hard and fast, it had almost taken his life. He'd been lucky, his second surgeon had told him, to only lose the lower part of his leg. Had they not caught it in time, it could have been worse.

In the end, it hadn't mattered. He'd retired from his job, because a half-man couldn't meet the physical requirements of a bounty hunter and bad guys didn't magically comply just because the dude hunting them was disabled. He'd lost his fiancé and submissive; not that Megan had ever said anything, but because he knew what she'd been thinking every time she'd crawled into bed beside him. He wasn't fit. He wasn't whole, how could he possibly make her submit when one of his legs ended in a fucking stump?

Oh, she'd tried to make it work. After four months, he'd finally released her just so he wouldn't have to endure it when she finally gave in to the inevitable and broke up with him.

He'd retired his membership from Black Light shortly after that. He didn't even go to watch anymore, because it wasn't watching that he wanted to do. He wanted to *touch*, god damn it. He wanted to get his hands all up in some hot, little submissive and wring gasp after moan after cry from her while he bent her to all of his basest desires. A half-man couldn't do that, and he'd be fucked up the ass before he let himself be objectified by some amputee fetishist, because that was the only reason anyone would let him top them at this point.

What was he doing here? Mentally, he had no doubt he was exactly what Pony needed, but physically? Why had he taken this job?

Spencer, that's why. Years ago, Black Light's grumpy, taciturn manager had been the only one stubborn enough to keep hounding after him after Marcus had shut everyone else out. Over the course of the eight months following his accident, he'd closed himself off from the world so effectively that all of his friends, his working acquaintances, even Megan had stopped coming by his house to check on him. And that Christmas, when he hit rock fucking bottom, who was it who showed up on his door not two seconds after he'd loaded his gun and just before he tucked the muzzle up under his chin?

Spencer. With a fucking fruit cake and a bottle of brandy.

They'd got drunk together, and for the first time Marcus bitched, and moaned, and even broke down and cried over his stupid, fucking leg. If he lived to be a thousand, he'd never forget what Spencer said to him: "Are you fucking done yet?"

Spoken in that bored 'what the hell are you complaining for' tone that he could have patented, he had it down so well.

Marcus had sat there, drunk, the awful taste of fruitcake in his mouth, and the realization slowly sinking into every recess of him that, yeah, he was done.

The next day, he'd woken up with the mother of all hangovers. He'd thrown away the fruitcake, unloaded the gun, ordered what would end up being the first out of the five prosthetics it took before he found one that fit him the best, and then he'd gotten back to living his life.

He was here today because Spencer had known a bottle of brandy at the right time might get him to open up and because he'd cared enough to tell him to get the fuck over himself at that dark moment when he'd needed most to hear it.

He owed the man. It grated, but he owed him.

Ever so slightly, Pony turned her head. She didn't look back at him, but it was enough for him to know she was past trying to ignore his presence. "Are you a dom?" she asked, her voice whisper soft.

"I was. Once upon a time. But don't go getting ideas," he wasted no time telling her. "Just because I was one doesn't mean I'm yours. I'm just a guy who knows the verbiage."

She looked down at her hands. After a moment, even more softly, she asked, "What's going to happen to me?"

The pale softness of her hair spilled in tangles down her back almost to her butt. It was pretty. She was pretty. Thin as she was, it wasn't hard to see how she might once have been beautiful.

"I'm going to take you home," he said gruffly. "I'm going to give you rules and then I'm going to teach you how to survive. You're going to learn how to do things for yourself again. You're going to dress yourself, cook for yourself, clean up, pay bills, work a job, make a decision—all of it."

She raised a hand to her face. He couldn't see for sure, but it wouldn't have surprised him if she'd just wiped away another tear.

"What if I don't want to?" she asked, her voice thick with countless more still unshed.

Marcus resisted the urge to rub his leg. It wasn't aching anymore, but he almost wished it would. It had been too long since he'd last had anyone hitting so many of his 'subby in need' triggers, but she was doing it. She was hitting them fast and hard, and the long-denied dom in him was fighting not to respond.

"Unfortunately, we don't get to make that choice," he told her. "We don't get to curl up our toes just because we lose someone, or our way of life." Or a leg. "We don't get to sulk. We don't get to cry. We sure as hell don't get to make it the problem of everyone else around us. Like it or not, the only thing we get to do is figure out how to keep going. You might very well hate me for it, but at least you'll get the chance to hate me outside of a mental hospital."

She looked back at him over her shoulder. "What about Puppy?"

"She's not your crutch. You don't get to lean on her anymore, and you sure as hell don't get to keep hurting her."

She flinched and quickly dropped her eyes to her hands.

"You don't get to keep hurting yourself either. Rule number one: No more self-harm. That rule starts on the honor system. Give me one reason to believe you've violated it and I'll strip your ass naked for inspections every day, multiple times a day, until you win my trust back again. Look at me."

He saw that order shiver through her. Almost as if against her will, she obeyed, locking her blue gaze with his steel gray one.

"I'm not a nice man, and I don't have a lot of patience. I

knew Ethen O'Dowell, and I know some of what you've had to do since he went to prison. I sympathize, but I'm not your dom. I don't love you, or cherish you, and I sure as hell won't put up with any manipulative attempts to top me from the bottom. I give the orders, you obey them; it's just that simple. Be a good girl and the next thirty days will go by as painlessly as I can possibly make them. Fight me, and I will make your life absolutely miserable in ways you can't possibly imagine right now."

"You'll punish me," she said flatly, no inflection in her voice.

"You weren't broken in the vanilla world," he confirmed. "You won't be fixed in it either." He could see the direction her thinking now wandered in, and he had to squash his inner dom before it could see this as a challenge to be immediately taken up. "Don't."

She didn't move. "Don't what?"

"Just. Don't. I'm not your master, but I'm not going to give you what you want either. I won't put you over my knee and spank your naughty bottom. In fact, I promise if you force my hand, you won't like a single one of the punishments I devise for you. Here's rule number two: in my house, there are no safewords. Earn it, you'll get it. It's that simple."

Her expression didn't change. Not only was she not scared, but his gut said she was going to test that just as fast as she could manage it. He wasn't surprised. She'd been punishing herself for months in what was, for all intents and purposes, a long-distance relationship. Her inner sub had to be desperate for the physical disciplinary contact of another. His dominant side twitched, only too happy to feed those needs. But, Marcus knew, he would need to tread carefully. He had no intention of becoming her next Ethen O'Dowell and thirty days from now, she would need to be able to take care of herself enough for the courts to deny the hospital's claim that she was incompetent. He had to get her ready so he could release her back into the world with a clear conscience. Then and only then, would he be able to retreat himself, obligation fulfilled, back into the quiet of his self-imposed isolation.

He couldn't afford to fall into the trap of thinking she was his, even if only temporarily. He certainly couldn't afford to fall into the trap of liking it.

He steeled himself. Pony was a victim in need of help, but she was also the enemy, and if he dared to let himself think about this any other way, then it would only make it that much harder in the end, when it came time to release her.

And he would. Because he didn't need any more problems and she certainly didn't need him.

CHAPTER 2

Pony/Anna

ony sat silently in the backseat of Marcus Hawke's maroon SUV. The child locks were engaged and there was a barrier of plexiglass between them. She suspected it might be bulletproof. There were rings tucked half-hidden between the seat cushions by the seatbelt buckles. She didn't know if that was added security for unruly passengers who had to be handcuffed, but there was also an eyebolt for ankle cuffs fixed into the floor between her feet. For kickers? She didn't know, but she wasn't struggling and she wasn't kicking, and she really didn't want to find out.

Or did she?

It was a forty-five-minute drive from Washington D.C. to Centreville, Virginia, where he lived in a two-story farmhouse on twenty secluded acres just off a quiet country road. The entire way there, she'd tried not to stare at him. Every time she did, he seemed to sense it and his gaze would find hers via the rearview mirror. Then her stomach would clench, her palms would sweat, and she'd quickly avert her eyes again. She rubbed her hands against her skirted thighs. Her head still hurt, but that wasn't what bothered her the most. It was the things he'd said at the hospital.

That he wasn't her Dom. Of course, he wasn't.

That he didn't love or cherish her. That had stung, though truly she should have been used to that.

That he wasn't above punishing her for her disobedience if she pushed him into it, and that he'd make sure she hated every bit of it. She wished she knew what his methods were. From the moment he'd threatened her, all she could think about was being punished. That was exactly what she needed, what she deserved for months' worth of failure, for being so inept and unlovable that Master Ethen's only avenue to be rid of her was to shoot her.

She stared out the window, watching as an old white farmhouse came into view beyond a freshly mowed pasture where round grass bales waited to be picked up. The old Virginian-style architecture with its peaked rooftops and wraparound porch was one of the nicest she'd seen, though not as nice as Master's home. It looked big. Much too big for just one person to live in. Two now, since she was here.

"Home sweet home," Marcus said, pulling up to the driveway. He clicked the garage opener on his visor, and then idled until the automatic door raised enough to let him ease into his parking space. He shut off the engine, then closed the door before unbuckling his belt. He looked at her in the rearview mirror again. "Are you going to give me trouble?"

She'd always worked so hard never to cause Master trouble, but Marcus wasn't Master. She shook her head.

"All right." He got out of the car and came around to let her out too. At the hospital, he'd walked her to the car with his hand on her elbow, put her in the back, and gave her the command to buckle her seatbelt. After only the smallest hesitation, she'd done it. Now here they were, in the privacy of his garage. Early spring in Virginia meant his garage was cold. She felt the coolness of the air moving up her legs from the moment he opened the door.

"Unbuckle your seatbelt," he told her.

She did it and then sat waiting, her back stiff, the fine hairs on her body prickling as she ached for him to command her to get out. Master wasn't even buried yet and here she was, in the home of another dom, not just following his commands but wishing for them.

She really was a traitor. A loyal submissive never would have come here so willingly. A submissive worth keeping would not now be waiting for Marcus's next command, all while contemplating disobedience just so she could bear the soothing, comfort of the punishment that might follow.

"Step out of the car."

She tried to hold herself immobile, but already her feet were moving to obey. Standing now between him and the car, she fisted her sweaty hands and swallowed convulsively. Her stomach was rolling. She felt sick in the pit of it.

"This way," he said, stepping aside. She followed him, two steps behind and a little to his right, halting when he stopped to close the car door, waiting until he started walking again so she could follow him into the house. She kept her head down, her posture perfect even though she no longer had her heels. She didn't have shoes at all. They must have fallen off her when she got shot and no one had thought to collect them before rushing her off to the hospital.

"Welcome to your new home," he said, opening the door from the garage into the kitchen. Dark wood cabinets clashed strikingly with stark white granite countertops and floor tiles. The appliances were silver. It was utterly clean, without so much as a stray cup on the dining table in the adjacent eating space or a spoon in the bottom of the double sink. "Wake up is at six sharp. I take my coffee black, no cream, no sugar, and you won't be making it. Breakfast is at eight, lunch at one, and dinner at seven. You won't be making those either. While you are here, you will take care of your own needs. You will do the chores that you are given. The more you progress, the more you'll be rewarded. Failure to progress will be met with consequences. Do you understand what I've just told you?"

"Yes, Sir."

His face didn't exactly harden, but his jaw clenched. His tone, however, was patient incarnate when he asked, "Are you my submissive?"

As if she needed the reminder. She fought not to wilt. "No, Sir."

His jaw clenched again. He shifted, clearing his throat before trying again.

"You are *not*," he emphasized, "my submissive. You aren't my employee, either. Don't call me sir. It's just yes or no. Do you understand?"

Every fiber in her rebelled. Her stomach rolled harder, knotting so violently she thought she might throw up. "Yes, Sir."

He studied her a moment, before tilting his head in a half-nod. "First test, first punishment, coming right up. Come with me."

Turning on his heel, he marched out of the kitchen.

Her deliberate disobedience didn't feel half as good as she'd thought it would. She followed him past the living room, down the hall and into a mostly empty cream-colored bedroom. The only furniture consisted of a four-drawer dresser and a double bed with a pale-yellow bedspread.

"Stand." He pointed to a spot in the middle of the floor.

She assumed her place and watched him leave. The minutes bled painfully by while the knots in her stomach grew tighter and tighter. Was he going to come back? Was this the punishment, being sent to her room and left there? The door was still open. She could hear his footsteps retreating further down the hall, and then nothing but silence. Her pounding heart thumped against her ribs, growing so intense that the dull ache in her head sharpened back into stabbing icepicks as she strained to pick up the slightest sound.

After only a few minutes, back down the hall he came, reappearing in her doorway carrying a full-sized medical scale. He muscled it over the threshold and set it on the floor in front of a narrow strip of bare wall by the empty closet.

"Strip to your underwear and get on." Turning, he walked out again, leaving her alone all over again.

She looked at the scale. Slowly, she removed her clothes, folding the ruined, blood-stained blouse and placing it on top of the dresser, hiding it under her neatly folded skirt. Naked, she returned to her designated spot.

She didn't have long to wait. Marcus reappeared in the doorway with a blank paper in one hand and thumbtack in his other. He froze when he saw her, and for just a blink, all she saw on his face was the dark disapproval of a dom who was done having his orders tested.

Only the vaguest hint of disapproval trickled down into his voice when he said, "I told you to strip *to your underwear.*"

"I don't have any, sir."

His hesitation was so slight it could barely be called that.

"Fine," he said, coming into the room with her anyway. He didn't look at her as he pinned the paper to the wall at face height directly in front of the scale. He then tied a pen on a string to the thumbtack. "Step on. Let's get a base weight for tomorrow."

If he thought this was a punishment, he could think again. There hadn't been a single week since Master had gone to prison that she hadn't been ordered to miss at least one day of meals. If he thought she was opposed to losing more weight, he was wrong. Master didn't allow fat on his menagerie girls, and she had long ago become the queen of never pinching so much as an inch of unwanted weight.

She stepped onto the scale, watching without interest as he adjusted the balancing arm.

"Eighty-four," he said, and then wrote that next to the date at the top of the pinned paper. "Either my scale or the hospital's is a little off. But it'll give us a base to work from. Stay here."

Taking her bloody clothes with him, again he walked out and when he returned it was with an old t-shirt and a pair of sweats. He tossed them at her from the doorway. "Put them on and meet me in the living room. If you're not there in five minutes, I'll add two smores and another movie to your punishment."

She startled. "Wh-what?"

"You heard me," he called back over his shoulder, already walking away.

Standing in the near-empty bedroom, she looked at the clothes in her hands. Sweats. Menagerie girls did not wear sweats. Menagerie girls didn't wear anything when at home with Master.

Marcus wasn't Master, and wasn't this all the very point he was trying right now to drill into her? Shoulders slumping, Pony crawled into the worn t-shirt and oversized pants. The elastic waist was too loose. She had to hold them up as she padded in bare feet back out to the living room.

"Couch," he ordered from the kitchen, where he had a bowl out on the counter already and was now busy digging through a drawer for silverware. He was making a dessert. Next to the bowl was an assortment of sauces—chocolate syrup, strawberry jam, nuts, whipped cream in a can, and maraschino cherries.

She was good in the kitchen. She always had been, although Puppy's mother had never allowed her to do any of the cooking or cleaning at her house. Not that Pony would have. Puppy's mother had hated her. That bitter old woman wasn't anyone's master either, not by a long shot. But the longer she stood watching Marcus in the kitchen doing what she ought to be, the stronger that long dormant desire to serve became. It itched up her spine and despite his order, she took a step toward him.

Closing the cupboard drawer, he pointed at her with the spoon he'd chosen. "Couch, right now or I'll add to your punishment."

Stomach dropping, skin itching, fingers tightening their grip on the waist of her too big pants, she went to the couch. Sit, he'd told her, but he hadn't told her where. Where did he like to sit? In the middle, on one of the ends? What if she took his preferred spot?

"One," he counted from the kitchen.

She began to panic, her breathing quickening, her chest heaving. "Where should I—"

"Two…"

"Where's your sp—"

"Three."

She sat, her whole body erupting into panic so sharp it cut through her veins like lightning. Perching in the middle of the couch, her feet drawn up under her, she heard his too-little, too-late tsk.

He took a bottle of caramel syrup out of the cupboard and set it next to the empty bowl. "Do you have any food allergies?"

"N-no," she stammered, so nervous she was shaking.

Pausing, he glanced at her. "Good girl, Anna."

She'd forgotten the 'sir'. Her stomach lurched, but the warmth of his unexpected praise slipped over her like a warm blanket. It settled the wildness of her badly shaking nerves, though she still shook as she watched him put the caramel back.

"Lactose intolerant?" he asked, getting a tub of vanilla ice cream out of the freezer.

"No." Sir! Her throat tightened, only just choking the word back. Her lips clamped, refusing to let her mouth speak it.

He watched her struggle not to say it for almost a full minute before the corner of his mouth curled into a faint smile. "Very good girl, Anna." He put the sprinkles away next. "If only I could put it all away, but that wouldn't get the point across, would it?"

She was going to be sick. She rubbed her stomach, the warmth of his praise both a balm upon her starving submissive's soul and a knife cutting her traitorous self to ribbons.

He scooped a single rounded ball of vanilla ice cream into the bowl, then topped it with a sprinkle of granola, an entire slice of banana, chocolate syrup, a spritz of whipped cream, a sprinkle of nuts, and finally a single bright red cherry.

He brought it to her, handing her the bowl first and then the spoon. He turned on the big television affixed to the wall above the fireplace mantle, signed in to Netflix and chose 'Chicken Little' off the kids' menu. Taking a blanket off the back of the couch, he draped it over her, tucking it in around her legs. "Comfortable?"

She couldn't remember the last time someone had asked her that. It was surprising how much she disliked it.

Without waiting for an answer, he turned the volume on the television up to a comfortable level. "You will eat every bite and you may not get off the couch until the movie is over."

She looked at the sundae. This was punishment?

He patted her on the knee. "Don't mind me. I'm going to go clean something."

That hit her surprisingly hard too. Like twin boring drills straight to the stomach. It hit her in shrill shocks of sensation that instantly tangled her and made her legs tense with the need to vault up off the couch and follow him back into the kitchen. He only got halfway before he suddenly veered toward the bathroom to fetch a box of tissues.

"Almost forgot," he said, tucking it up against her hip. "You're going to need those."

To watch Chicken Little, eat a sundae, and sit on the couch? She watched him walk away, wanting with all her might to call after him, "Don't make me laugh!" Except she wasn't laughing. She wasn't crying, either, but there was no denying the awfulness of the tension vibrating in her knotted stomach. The knots were stranglingly tight as he took a clean cloth from a drawer, wet it in the sink and then began cleaning countertops.

Pony clutched her bowl. She hadn't been able to clean anything since Master went to prison. She hadn't so much as made her own bed when she'd stayed at Puppy's house. It had felt so wrong, as if there was no point. This… watching Marcus do what she couldn't and hadn't been able to do in so very long, and which she yearned to do with all the passion in her breast, hit her hard.

"Eat," Marcus reminded, turning his attention to washing the cupboard doors next.

She looked at her ice cream, just now beginning to melt in her bowl.

This was stupid. Marcus was not her master and his was not the house she wanted most to take care of, as if it were an extension of the man she'd loved with all her heart. That man was gone. So was his house, for that matter.

This was really, really stupid.

She fixed her attention on the television with its animated chicken running around on the screen. Her stomach was hollow in that empty-pinching way she had long ago come to like because nothing tasted as good as obeying Master felt.

Except he was gone now and she'd never feel it again.

Marcus wasn't her Dom, but he had given her an order and he was expecting to be obeyed, and surely that was better than this limbo of abandonment that she'd been living in for the past eight months.

She tried to eat, but it was awful. It tasted like failure and incompetence. It tasted exactly the way it ought to for a sub who was sitting on her ass, tucked into a blanket on the couch while someone else was busily working around her.

He was sweeping now, the whispering brush of the broom over the floor tiles scratching all the way up her prickling spine until she couldn't bear it. She would never, ever have just sat by while Master cleaned. Not that he would have, the house was her responsibility. Failure to keep it up to his impossible-to-achieve level of standards resulted in punishment every time, and God knows Master was the king of terrible punishments. Piggy had her wallow—that cold, filthy mud hole that he'd made her kneel in whenever she'd displeased him. Puppy had her kennel and Kitty that claustrophobic cage under his bed where she used to wail, kick and cry, and sometimes even piss herself before he'd let her out. But she—Pony shuddered—she was easy. For her, he had never needed anything more creative than a whip-thin crop and a bondage bench to secure her over.

Pony hated pain. She couldn't take much of it without breaking down completely, not that that had ever tempered Master's hand or saved her from the full measure of his wrath. It hadn't tempered her own hand either. Each time he'd condemned her to whip strokes to punish her inability to keep Puppy under control, she'd dealt them using her own leash and she'd beaten her own back or legs just as hard as she could. She'd done it until she'd convinced herself that there was comfort in the pain—it meant he still wanted her enough to try to teach her to do better.

Where was that comfort now? Gone, that's where. And this was what she was reduced to. Sitting on a stranger's couch, watching TV with ice cream melting in her bowl and the taste of it lingering like ash in her mouth.

She couldn't hold still. Kicking out of the blanket, she tried to get up but she couldn't think what to do with the bowl taking up her hands. She had a choice—the coffee table, the end table to her left with its vintage multi-colored Tiffany lamp, or the floor.

"Butt on the sofa," Marcus said, his tone and expression both stone-hard. "This is a punishment and you will stay right there until it's over."

Pony stayed, hunkered on the sofa, melting ice cream in hand, unable to eat, unable to disobey, unable to just sit here, listening in growing franticness while he did her jobs. He dusted when he was done sweeping, moving silently through the living room around her, making careful effort not to obstruct her view of the show but certainly not hiding either. And it was killing her.

"You may not help me," he said when he got to the end table and she tried to lift the lamp so he could dust under it. "You're also not eating. I expect that bowl to be empty by the end of the show. You've got forty minutes."

Or what, the defiant part of her brain fought to demand. He'd make her cookies? She'd have to watch another cartoon? This was the *stupidest* punishment she'd ever heard of!

She glared at her bowl, her eyes stinging with the threat of unshed tears until he came and sat down on the coffee table directly in front of her.

"I will not be topped from the bottom," he said flatly. "When and if I decide you require discipline, you can bank on the fact that I will not spank your naughty bottom until you're a sorry little girl. I won't wash out your mouth with soap, or send you to the naughty corner, or make you write 'I will not' lines until your fingers fall off. I am not your Dom. You are not my sub. You will obey me because you are living in my house while I try to help you out of the mess you're in. If you decide not to obey, then I will force the issue, but I promise I will find a way to do it that you will not like. It won't feed the fantasy. It won't feed your soul. If you wait until your sundae is a melted mess, it won't look or taste appealing and I will still make you eat it. Do we understand one another?"

She hated him. She hated this place. She hated her inability to just get up and march out of his house. She couldn't think as far as what consequences were sure to follow that—from court, to hospital, to him, to the sweatpants she had to hold hiked up around her hips or they'd fall down—nothing mattered. Nothing made sense.

She was breaking inside, splintering cracks that were cutting her to pieces and releasing the tears she was trying so hard to fight back. Covering her eyes with her hand, she hung her head.

"Every bite," he said ruthlessly. "Eat, Anna."

She would sooner drop the bowl on the floor in front of him, making the biggest mess she could, which she would then have to watch him clean up—this was horrible.

Shoulders jerking, she began to cry. Hating herself, she put a dripping spoonful of sundae soup in her mouth. It was sweet and chocolaty, and it tasted every bit as awful as the punishment it was meant to be.

When he was done dusting, he returned to the kitchen to make dinner: potato and ham casserole. Every chop of the knife's blade skimming the cutting board made her heart hurt and her feelings of ineptitude grow.

"You still have three bites left," he noted when Chicken Little hit the end of its credits and he ventured out of the savory-smelling kitchen to check on her. Her nose was running, her face was wet with tears, and her head hurt so much she could barely see. She hadn't touched the tissues he'd given her. He shook his head once, as if he really felt sorry about it before declaring, "I was going to allow you to help me set the table, but your behavior right now doesn't warrant a reward."

The sight of his broad back as he walked away from her, heading back into the kitchen snapped her out of her helpless misery. She lobbed her bowl after him, hitting him squarely in the back. The bowl bounced off and shattered when it hit the floor, sending the spoon and porcelain shards scattering, but she barely noticed. Her attention was locked entirely on her own unhappiness and the sudden about-face that Marcus executed, before he came striding back to her.

She thought he was going to grab her by the neck. He didn't. He caught just under her jaw, with the heat of his palm burning into the skin of her throat. It wasn't a tight grip. All she had to do was step back and she'd have easily escaped him, but that look on his face was anything but escapable. If only he would squeeze, instead of oil on the fire of her unhappiness, the tightening of his authoritative hand would have made her feel better. It would have comforted and calmed her. But no, he had her in his hand, and his grip kept loose enough for her to easily escape.

She didn't know how close she was to just bursting into tears until it happened.

Get mad, she wanted to scream right into his face. Shake her, yell! He was frowning at her, but why wasn't he throwing her to the ground and whipping off his belt so she could crawl and writhe and scream desperate apologies between the cracks of his angry lashes. Why wasn't he hurting her? Master would have.

Very calmly, Marcus growled, "Don't. Hit. Me, Anna. I will

never strike you out of anger and never without your consent; I expect that same courtesy out of you. Don't ever do that again, and I mean ever. Got it?"

Sick to her stomach, unable to stop the tears now pouring from her so hard that she could barely breathe through the shoulder wracking sobs, she did what Master would never have allowed. She stepped back.

Just as she'd thought it would, Marcus's hand did not tighten its grip. He let her go. Every so slightly, his stone-gray eyes narrowed, but he let go.

She backed from him on shaking legs. He took a step, but then stopped. His jaw clenched once, but he did not pursue her any further.

Turning, feeling only the mounting sin of disobedience heaping down upon her, she made herself walk away. There was nowhere to go except back down the hallway to the room with the scale. Which one was it again? She stopped, confused.

"First door on the right after the bathroom," Marcus grimly called, stalking her only as far as the mouth of the hallway.

She went into her room. Dare she close the door? Her hand shook, but she did it. And then backed away until the backs of her knees bumped up against the edge of the double bed and she collapsed on it, unable to stop crying, just waiting. Master would have beaten her unconscious for daring half of what she had done in the last ten minutes alone.

After a moment, she heard Marcus's footsteps retreating back into the kitchen. It was maybe a minute before the soft chop of the knife and clatter of dishes signaled his calm return to cooking.

Because he wasn't her Dom. He didn't care what she did. He didn't care, period.

She'd lost the only person in the world who had cared.

Cared enough to house her, to command her, to fuck her, and to hurt her when the desire for it settled into him.

Master Ethan was gone and nothing could have been more clear to her than the now driving realization that she would never have that back. She would never belong to anyone the way she had to him.

She was lost.

She was alone.

And it would never, ever get any better than this.

CHAPTER 3

Pony/Anna

She couldn't take it.

Her stomach cramped so hard it hurt, and then she threw up. It happened every bit as unexpected as the sobbing tears that just wouldn't stop, giving her no time even to run to the bathroom.

She stared, appalled at the mess on the carpet between her feet. She'd just ruined it because she couldn't take her punishment.

This was why Master had shot her.

This was why no one wanted her.

Menagerie girls were allowed neither to dress or undress themselves without permission, but she took off her ill-fitting sweatpants and tried to clean up what she'd done. The fabric wasn't as absorbing as she needed it to be and the regurgitated chocolate was staining.

Yet again, she was failing. Incompetent.

Useless.

She couldn't stay here. She didn't want to be anywhere in this house when Marcus found out what she'd done.

She tried the window only because Marcus would see her if she went out the door. Never in a million years did she think it would actually open to her. None of Master's windows had opened, and at Puppy's house, the bedroom window had been nailed shut before Pony came home. But the moment Pony tried the latch, the old turn-out hinges rolled open.

Cold air rushed in, stinging her bare skin, but that wasn't about to stop her. In only an oversized t-shirt now, she popped out the screen and crawled outside.

The grass was stiff with frost. Within steps, the icy cold had turned to knives under her bare feet, but terrified by what she was doing and the great unknown that accompanied the inevitability of getting caught, she ran all the way from the house to the old red barn standing sentry in the pasture beside Marcus's house.

From the tidiness inside, she could only guess that Marcus owned this structure too. There were no horses or livestock of any kind. It smelled of clean dirt, leather, old straw, and wood. The interior was set up like a workshop, with stacks of wood planks on pallets against one wall and worktables laden with tools on the other. She could smell the assortment of stains in the cans neatly arranged on a heavy-duty steel shelf. A half-finished china cabinet stood in the center of it all, patiently awaiting the finishing touches yet to be applied around the trim. Two rustic lawn chairs were assembled but not yet stained on another pallet. A freshly stained paddle with the words 'Daddy's Tool' dangled on a hook from one of three short loops of rope from the ceiling rafter.

Right up until she saw them, her only plan was to be somewhere other than the house for that awful span of time when Marcus decided he was ready to confront her about her living-room disobedience only to discover what she'd done in the bedroom. But standing here, in the midst of all this orderly creation, all she could feel was the burden she had become. Unwanted, unloved.

Destructive, combative. Disobedient.

She didn't want to be here anymore, but there was no way out and no way for any of this to get better. Ever.

One minute she was standing in the cold doorway, the dying light of day illuminating those two empty loops of rope, and in the next she had the stool from near the worktable thunked down on the ground under one of them and she was climbing up to grab the rope. She pulled the rope down far enough to untie the loop. She had no idea how to make a noose, so she wrapped it twice around her neck and tied a knot.

Zero thought went into this beyond one: At least she'd get to see Master again.

Zero hesitation went into it, either. She had to arch up on tiptoes in order to reach the hook. She tied the other end of the rope to that. She didn't bother wondering whether or not it was going to hurt before she kicked the stool out from under herself.

Her drop was maybe four inches and her neck didn't break. She dangled, the rope cutting into her skin as she first gasped and choked, and then began to struggle as she realized she could still breathe, just not enough. And yes, this did hurt. In true Pony fashion, she'd botched this and it wasn't going to end quickly.

She clawed at the rope, trying to pull herself up so her own weight wasn't killing her. It was impossible. Her arms didn't have the strength.

What the hell was she doing?

The pounding of her heartbeat in her ears was deafening.

Pinpricks of light were bursting behind her eyes. She couldn't get her fingernails under where the rope was cutting into her neck and all she could think about was how furious Master would be because she was damaging his property.

She was his to hurt, his to kill. Apparently.

...Really?

After everything she'd done for him?

After four years of serving him, faithfully, selflessly. She'd humiliated herself for him, and humiliation had never been her kink. She worked jobs she'd hated for him and after he went to prison, she'd been so ashamed over her inability to function enough to hold onto that awful job that she'd ended up waiting tables—or at least, she'd tried—just so he could have money in his commissary account.

She'd gone without food, without clothes, without comfort, for over a year, because of him.

And how did he thank her? He'd tried to put a bullet in her head. The *back* of her head. He'd been too much of a coward even to look her in the eyes while he betrayed her loyalty and trust to that last enth of a degree.

That motherfucking son of a bitch.

The rope snapped, dropping Pony into a heap in the dirt. No longer strangling on her own body weight, she clawed the rope loose enough to draw her first deep gasp of air. Her aching throat rebelled, and she doubled over coughing until she was raw from it.

She was only just beginning to catch her breath again when the door to the barn suddenly yanked open and the light inside snapped on. Marcus took one look at her and fury exploded across his face.

She struggled to get up before he reached her, but her limbs weren't working right. He grabbed the length of rope off the floor, and the hair at the back of her head, hauling her up off the ground. He looked at her neck, her legs, and swung her around. Limping heavily, he marched her back to the house.

The grass was even colder and sharper against the bottoms of her bare feet on the trip back. When she stumbled, he grabbed her arm and suddenly the whole world flipped upside down as he ducked to sling her over his shoulder. By the time they got back to the house, she was shivering, and he was limping badly.

Still, he carried her through the kitchen, past the living room and straight to the bathroom. He set her down in the bottom of the tub.

"Strip," he ordered. Turning the faucet on, he adjusted the temperature of the water, waiting only just long enough for her to crawl out of her shirt before he switched the shower on. He took her shirt from her, grabbed her by the hair and marched her under the full force of the spray. "Where's your damn pants?" he demanded.

Not waiting for an answering, he left the bathroom.

Pony stood under the spray until her skin stopped reading the lukewarm heat of the water as scaldingly hot. Her shivering eased, but she was still trembling. Hanging her head, her throat so tender she could barely swallow, she waited for him to come storming back.

It felt a small eternity before he returned and when he did, he wasn't angry anymore. He came back to the shower and just looked at her.

Shaking too hard to keep her posture perfect, pretty sure it didn't matter anymore anyway, Pony hugged herself and waited to be condemned.

Marcus didn't speak. After a moment, he put his fingers into the water above her head, then bent to adjust the temperature, making it warmer. When he was done, he drew the shower curtain between them, but he didn't leave. Sitting down on the closed toilet instead, he said, "Do you want to wash up?"

She shook her head, only belatedly realizing he couldn't see that through the curtain. "N-no, s-s-sir," she rasped, wincing and catching her throat. "I-I mean… no, Marcus."

He let the slip go. "Wash up, Anna."

Finding a bar of soap on a set of corner shower shaver racks, she lathered up both her hands and washed herself.

"Do you want to wash your hair?"

She hesitated in the midst of rinsing. "Do… do you want me to wash my hair?"

"What I want is for you to acknowledge that the last time you washed your hair was long enough ago that it needs it again."

Menagerie girls weren't allowed to wash themselves without permission any more than they were allowed to dress themselves. While her master had been in prison, they'd gotten around that order by showering together and washing each other. Puppy had washed her hair last. What had that been, two days ago?

What had it been since she'd last washed her hair without Ethan allowing it?

She shuffled around on legs that still felt unsteady, found the shampoo and began lathering up her hair. She didn't know Dove made a shampoo for men only. The smell of menthol wafted on the steam as she rubbed her scalp, the short hair feeling spiky and gathering the longer strands until it was piled in suds on her head. She didn't feel clean so much as she felt as if she were getting away with something terrible and wrong.

That Marcus remained sitting in the room with the shower curtain pulled a little more than halfway closed, didn't bother her. Her body, clothed or not, hadn't been hers for so long that neither privacy nor nudity registered anymore.

"Rinse," he told her, and she did.

Backing up under the spray, she let the warm water pour over her. The trail of suds slipped over her skin, caressing her small breasts like whisper-soft fingertips. The coil of her long hair followed the pouring water off her head to spill down her back until the tips brushed the swells of her ass.

"Conditioner next."

It had been so long since anyone had commanded her like this. Stepping out from under the full rain of the showerhead, she applied conditioner to her hair and worked it in. It was falling out, but then it had been for months. No longer the thick, full mane she once had been proud to be admired for, her hair was so thin that it had become hard to pull back into her customary ponytail without showing swaths of bare scalp. As careful as she could, she combed the conditioner in with her fingertips, but she still lost a lot to the gentle pull of the water. The drain was starting to clog and the bottom of the tub was filling up with water, now rising over the tops of her feet.

"I'm sorry," Marcus said.

Pony stopped. She wanted to look out at him, to see if he'd really just said that to her, but he'd drawn the shower curtain and she didn't want to challenge his will.

"Did you hear me?"

"Yes—" Her sore throat convulsed and she stammered as, needing desperately to fill that void where 'sir' ought to go, she added, "Marcus."

"I'm sorry," he repeated again. "A few years back before I retired, I had a girl with an eating disorder. What I did tonight was one of the punishments I used to give her. Well... the sundae. Not the movie or the couch, or the cleaning," he added, his tone taking on a vaguely amused note. "She wasn't a service submissive." That thin note of amusement was gone when he added, "And you're not an anorexic with a body image disorder. I did not mean to make you sick and if that was the catalyst for what sent you out to the barn, then I am truly, deeply sorry."

It was and it wasn't. Pony looked at the white tile wall dead ahead of her, with no idea of what to say. She ought to apologize too, but she couldn't make herself do it.

"I'd like to start over."

She looked at the shadow of him through the curtain, her stomach already tightening.

"We have thirty days to get you ready to counter the hospital and the State's claim that you can't be trusted to take care of yourself and that hospitalization or an assigned legal guardian is your best solution. I've been that guardian. I know exactly what it entails, so believe me when I say you don't want to have to live like that. Not if you can help it. So, I'm going to ask you a question and I want you to consider your answer carefully. Were I to offer my dominance long enough for you to learn how to shut out his voice and develop your own, would that help you or would that only make things worse?"

Frozen under the spray, Pony hardly daring to breathe much less move. "I don't understand."

After a brief heartbeat of silence, the shadow of Marcus on the other side of the shower curtain stood up and faced her. "Look at me."

Did he want her to move the curtain or lean over far enough to look at him around the edge? Her chest heaved as she quickly tried to calculate the consequence for choosing the wrong one. Her hand shook, but she slipped a few inches sideways and peeked around the curtain.

"Do you," Marcus asked her pointedly, "need a dom to help you get through this? We can set this up as a mentorship, or I could top you. Or I could make a phone call to a friend or two, masters with many years of experience if you're not comfortable with me doing it."

Comfortable? She stared at him, not understanding why that was a concern and afraid to trust what she thought this offer might mean. "I-I-I don't..."

"Kneel," he told her.

She knelt, the spray of the shower hitting her in the head. She stared straight at him, ignoring it.

"Stand."

She stood.

"Did your master ever ask you to present?"

Regularly in the beginning, but towards the end he hadn't as much. "Yes, Marcus."

"If I asked you to present, what would you do?"

Her body responded faster than she could formulate the words. She braced her feet a shoulder's width apart. Back straight, she pushed her breasts out and parted the shielding folds of her sex with her fingertips to bare herself in the most vulnerable way a woman could. She was furry down there. Shamefully, embarrassingly furry. She should have shaved when Puppy told her to, but she'd been so angry and so depressed. And so stubbornly dead set against obeying anything Puppy or her man told her to do because neither of them were her master.

She held her furry self open for his inspection, the slow burn of shame rising up through her belly to scald her face. He didn't even look down. That burned worse, because of course he wouldn't be interested in the disobedient, unkempt submissive who, on her first day in his home, had made two messes and then tried to kill herself.

She kept her shoulders back, but inside she was wilting.

Marcus took a step closer to the tub, his gaze locked on her eyes. "What can I do to you, Anna?"

She blinked, not at all understanding and when she

opened her mouth to say 'anything' he raised a hand, cutting her off.

"Let me rephrase, what can I *not* do to you?"

That was even more baffling.

"What are your hard limits?"

She was a Menagerie girl. She wasn't allowed to have any.

"Can I spank you?"

"Yes, Sir."

"Cane you? Six of my hardest strokes, no warmup. Right here, right now."

Prickling dread crawled its way up the backs of her legs and across her buttocks, but she knew better than to clench. "Yes, Sir."

"Fuck six," he said gruffly, and moved a step closer. "Twenty. You'll wear the bruises for a week and I guarantee I'll break the skin. You'll bleed for me. Can I do that?"

Her throat convulsed, but she didn't hesitate. "Yes, Sir."

"Lie down in the bottom of the tub so I can piss on you."

Pony lay down on her back, her only flinch being against the stray drops of water now hitting her face.

"Open your mouth. I'm going to shit in it."

Her stomach churned, tears stinging her eyes, but she opened her mouth.

He didn't move, but his voice grew harsher. "On your belly. I'm going to sodomize you with the biggest cock I can find."

She turned onto her belly, burying her face in her arms. Her nipples were peaked, and her thighs shaking. There wasn't anything pleasurable in what he was saying, but it had been so long since she'd been commanded. She didn't want to be anyone's toilet, but at least he was willing to use her. She didn't know if she could take being caned until her flesh split under the lashes, but she'd hold herself as still for it as she could manage and thank him for every stroke. It would be worth it if only he'd tell her 'good girl, well done' when it was over.

"Stand up, look at me." He sounded disappointed and he hadn't even touched her yet.

What had she done wrong? She got up, water dripping off her head onto her face. She didn't bother to wipe it away. She hung her head.

"Look at me."

Swallowing hard, she met his stare.

"Tell me one thing I may not do to you."

She shook her head, her mind an absolute blank. Tell him no? It wasn't her place. What he wanted, whatever he needed, it was her place to provide not to deny.

"That's what I thought," he said grimly. "You can't consent, Anna, if you can't tell me no." His jaw clenched once and then relaxed, but his expression was never anything but stern. "Finish your shower. I want every part of you clean, head to toe. Turn the water off, dry yourself, put your shirt back on, and meet me back in the living room."

He left and with it went that thin, fragile hope that she'd only just begun to harbor that someone might find her useful again.

She broke down in useless tears, her sore throat choking her as she tried not to make any sound. Helpless to do anything else, she also did as he'd instructed. She didn't know if 'head to toe' meant shaving, but there was a razor in the shower and she put it to good use. Her hands shook, especially at first when all she could think about was if it wouldn't be easier on everyone if she just cut her wrists.

That feeling of hanging in the barn haunted her, though, and that suicidal thought never birthed beyond a flitting thing —there and just as quickly discarded. She shaved, she cried, and then she got out, dried off, dressed, and made her way back out to the living room exactly as she'd been told.

Marcus was in the kitchen, pulling a glass casserole dish out of the oven. She could smell savory potatoes, ham and cheese, and her stomach cramped.

"Sit down," he said without more than a glance at her. "Pick up the pen, I want you to write something down."

Her long hair dripping water down her back of her borrowed t-shirt, Pony approached the table as if it were a coiled snake, ready to strike. She looked at the paper waiting for her, but it was blank.

Sinking into the chair, she picked up the pen, then looked at him.

"One," he began to dictate. "Wake up, six a.m. Weigh in, bathroom, dress, make coffee."

Pony obediently wrote it down, a tiny pinprick of startlement bursting in her gut as she brought each word into tangible being in black ink and her own painstakingly neat penmanship.

"Two, 6:15 am, exercise." Marcus dished the casserole up into two white bowls. "Three, shower and dress for the day. Tomorrow we'll go shopping and I'll pick you up a few things. It won't be Bloomingdale's, but you'll be covered. You don't have to write that last part."

Pony stopped and obediently crossed out the few words she'd written after 'dress for the day.' She waited, pen poised for him to start again.

"Four," he said, coming to the table to set a bowl beside her before sitting down at the head of the table. "Set the table for breakfast and serve."

Pony froze mid word, and stared. Serve? He wanted her to serve? Had she heard him wrong? Maybe he was joking. She glanced up to find him staring straight back at her, the stoniness of his expression saying clearly the man had never told a joke in his life. He absolutely knew what he was offering her and her stomach flipped, her heart stumbling in her chest. "Y-you want... me?"

"I do the cooking," he said, ignoring her question. "I drink coffee until noon and after that, I prefer iced tea. Twist of lemon, no sugar. There should always be a pitcher in the refrigerator. You're not writing this down."

Snapping her mouth shut, she quickly bent her head to write.

"You're not eating either," he noted. "Can you not do two things at once? If I respect you enough to cook for you, should you not respect me enough not to let it get cold?"

She took a hasty bite and kept writing. Two chews in, the flavor hit her tongue and she froze all over again. The portion he'd given her was slightly less than half what he'd served himself. The potatoes were soft, the ham savory, and the vegetables and cheese perfectly blended. The warmth settled gently into her empty stomach, heating her from the inside out.

"Still feeling sick?"

She shook her head, touched that he would even bother himself to ask. "No, Sir."

"Was it a stress response or too much sugar, do you think?"

Her stomach was so used to being empty these days, half the time she threw up the first time she tried to eat anyway. She bowed her head, not wanting to lie, but not wanting to answer either.

"When you're done eating, I want you to do the dishes while I clean your room."

She jumped, staring at him again only now appalled. "No, please, I can do it."

"My house, my rules," he said flatly. "It's also my error of judgment that caused it in the first place, so I'll clean it up. Did you just argue with me?"

Her face burned hotter. She quickly bowed her head. "I'm sorry, Sir."

"Don't apologize for doing what I want you to do."

Flustered, Pony knew better than to trust that too. He didn't want her to argue, no dominant wanted his submissive to argue with him. But how many times now had he said he wasn't her Dom, and yet what was she doing right now but writing down his expectations of her.

Leaning back in his chair with a sigh, Marcus wiped his mouth on a napkin and pushed his half-finished bowl aside. "I'm not O'Dowell," he said grimly. "You're not in that relationship anymore, you aren't bound by those rules. This is a new relationship, a new set of rules, and you just expressed a personal preference so that I would know what you really think and feel. I think that deserves a reward."

Ethen didn't care what her personal preferences were and he definitely would not have rewarded her for expressing one. Practically able to feel the stinging slap that ought to be coming, Pony put her pen down and braced herself for the trick concealed within his promised treat.

"What kind of reward?" she asked cautiously.

Holding up a staying finger, Marcus got up from the table. "Wait right here."

Nervous panic fluttered inside her, but there was no quick smack to the back of her head as he passed behind her on his way to disappear down the hall. He returned a few minutes later with a pair of leather wrist cuffs, padded in soft red velvet on the inside and connected together by a two-link chain.

Her stomach tightened all over again, her breath catching in the back of her throat. Her nipples tightened into instant peaks. She quickly averted her eyes, trying not to let her eagerness show. He wasn't going to put those on her. That was ridiculous. Not for arguing. Especially since she wasn't his.

She wasn't anybody's anymore, and no matter how much she wished she could be, that wasn't going to change. Especially not with Marcus.

CHAPTER 4

Pony/Anna

"*L*et me see your eyes," Marcus commanded as he dropped the leather cuffs on the table between them and sat back down in his chair.

She tried not to, but she couldn't help shivering as she looked at them. Almost desperately, she latched her gaze onto his and forced herself to hold it, despite the acrobatics of her racing heart and twisting, knotting stomach.

"Scared?" he asked.

Afraid she might burst into tears if she tried speaking out loud, she shook her head.

"No," he agreed. "You're close to crying, but not because you're scared. How long has it been, honey?"

"Almost a year," she whispered through a too-tight throat.

He grunted. "Stand up."

She knocked the chair back in her haste to obey, the clumsy sound of it threw her even more off-kilter. Menagerie girls weren't supposed to do that. Menagerie girls were sedate, elegant, and graceful in their obedience. They didn't knock over chairs or allow their furniture to scrape the floor tiles the way she'd just done, but Marcus didn't seem to notice. She waited, hands at her sides, her damp palms pressed tightly against her t-shirt clad thighs.

Picking up the cuffs, he beckoned her to him.

Her legs were shaking again. So was the rest of her. Half-expecting this still to be a trick, she crept to stand before him.

He twirled his finger, motioning her to turn around.

Her breaths quickened. Of all the many things that could happen to a girl when her back was turned to a man, only some of them were nice. The rest could be quite terrible.

Well-practiced at learning to expect the terrible, Pony turned her back. Her skin prickled, every fine hair rising to stand on end as she waited to be touched. Nobody touched her anymore. Only Puppy and only because Ethen had gone to prison. And because Pony had stood over her, bullying her, refusing to allow her friend the chance to break away and finally find a measure of happiness in the arms of another Dom.

Pony flinched from the caress that, instead of taking hold of her arms or wrist, brushed the small of her back.

"Shh," Marcus soothed, the coolness of his tone making her skin flush hot.

She braced herself, head down, fists clenched tight, determined not to move again.

Warm and flat, his palm settled against her spine. He rubbed gently upward as far as her shoulders. Her small breasts grew heavier, her nipples swelling beneath the scraping fabric of her t-shirt as she breathed.

Gathering her damp hair, he divided the long strands before twisting them into a loose braid. By the time he finally did take gentle hold of her wrist, her breath was as shaky as her knees.

"Your safeword is red, same as any club."

She didn't care what he did to her, she'd cut out her own tongue before she stopped this with a safeword.

One at a time, he buckled her wrists behind her back in the comforting embrace of each cuff. He might just as well have burritoed her in a warm blanket and tucked her safely into bed. Calm like she hadn't felt in far too long washed through her.

"Too tight?"

She shook her head, not that she'd have cared if they were. She could feel his finger running along the seam despite her assurance, checking for himself to make sure her circulation was not restricted.

"All right," he said, satisfied. "Sit back down."

He patted her bottom as she stepped away, and it was such an offhand and yet proprietary thing for him to do. Like he did it to her all the time.

Liquid warmth pooling in her belly spilled lower, tickling her pussy lips as she moved to take her seat. For the first time in well over a year—since before Piggy ran away, in fact—it felt as if life had just returned to normal.

"Obviously, you won't be able to write, so…" Reaching across the table, he took both her pen and paper and began to fill in the rest of her schedule of expectations. "Five, dinner is at seven. I'll cook, you'll set the table and"—he looked at her—"if you're good, you may serve."

Fluttering spasms, the closest thing to arousal that she'd felt in almost a year rippled through her sex. Her breath caught against her will, her face growing hot all over again.

"Six," he continued, seemingly unaware of the blossoms his calm authority was so effortlessly unfurling in her core. "What we're going to do won't be easy for you. I don't expect perfection, but I do expect you to try. Good behavior will win you rewards. Bad behavior will result in a loss of privileges. Do I need to cut your reward short so you can eat? I didn't cook for you so it could grow cold."

Pony looked down at her bowl. She couldn't hold her fork any more than she could hold a pen, but that didn't seem to bother Marcus. Honestly, it didn't bother her either. She'd been offered a return to normal and she took it, eagerly. It might not last. Tomorrow he might change his mind again and be right back to *I am not your Dom*.

Scrambling up to half kneel in her chair gave her the leverage she needed to catch the edge of her bowl with her teeth and pull it closer toward her. She'd have stuck her face in it, eating like a dog if that's what he wanted. He was commanding her, and she could have cried she'd missed this so much.

"No, no, no," he said, freezing her before she could snag that first hot bite. Her heart stumbled to a stop with the rest of her. The sting of tears hit the back of her eyes as she prayed he wasn't so sadistic as to bring her this close just to yank her dream back out from under her. "Dogs eat in dog dishes on the floor and they need all four paws to do it. Are you a dog, Anna?"

She was Pony. She shook her head.

He held out his hand. "Give me your bowl."

He was. He was taking it away from her. One would have thought as much as she'd cried, she would be all out of tears, but she had to blink hard to fight back a fresh wave. Bowing her head, she carefully picked up the bowl with her teeth and, climbing out of her seat, navigated it into his waiting hand.

"Good girl," he said, and her grieving heart fluttered. "Sit down."

Disappointment and gratitude cut her through her in

equal measures. At least he'd given her that before he took it all away.

"Did I say turn away from me?" he asked when she started back to her waiting chair. "We're not done. We've only just started, in fact."

She looked at him and then her chair. Afraid this might be devolving into another punishment and even more afraid that asking for clarification would take it there faster, Pony started to lower herself to her knees at his feet.

"No," he stopped her again. "Sit here." Shifting his chair so it faced her rather than the table, Marcus adjusted himself a little straighter in his seat and then patted his lap. "Facing me, please."

Please, no less. Her stomach knotted, but her heart quickened. The hungering need to be a good girl—anybody's good girl—carried her right to his knee. It was dampened only a little by the inner voice that whispered what a traitor she was to like it this much. He put his steadying hand on her hip while she eased herself down to perch on his hard thighs. Her master wasn't even buried yet and here she was, not just doing this but wanting it.

She swallowed convulsively, but it wasn't just her mouth watering when he picked up her bowl and dished up a bite. He brought it to his lips and she automatically tightened her stomach muscles to muffle its hollow rumble. She didn't want to diminish his pleasure while he ate her supper in front of her.

Except he didn't.

Blowing gently, he offered it to her.

Her chest rose and fell so fast. There was a trick here somewhere. She wanted it too much, so there had to be. But when she opened her mouth, he fed her.

As if she were precious.

She broke down, so grateful that she almost couldn't chew through the keening sobs.

"Don't force yourself to eat when you're full, even if I ask you to," Marcus told her, feeding her another bite just as soon as she swallowed the last. "If your stomach hurts, I want to know. If you get sick, I want to know. If you feel you have to make yourself sick, I definitely want to know, and I don't care what I'm doing at the time. You're to tell me immediately. If I'm busy, disturb me. If I'm asleep, wake me up. That's an order."

She nodded, chewing and crying and trying so hard to pull herself back together. She was a horrible submissive, making this all about herself. If she were really grateful, she'd be doing everything she could to make this fun and sexy for him. As it was, it was everything she could do just not to be a snotty, sniveling mess.

Picking up a napkin, Marcus put it to her nose and told her to blow. Then fed her until her bowl was empty and her stomach was anything but hollow. It cramped, she was so full. She didn't say anything. She wasn't about to ruin this, not for anything.

"Do you want more?" he asked, scraping the last cheesy bite out of the bowl and offering it to her.

She didn't, but she'd have kept eating for as long as he wanted to keep doing this. Did he want to keep doing it, though? Or was he only asking to be polite before moving on to what he really wanted to do? She hadn't known many overtly polite Doms, but he had said please. To her, no less.

"No, thank you, Sir." She really was horrible. Just saying that word had her belly warming in all those old familiar ways that once made the thought of being some man's submissive the sexiest, most seductive thing in existence. She'd thought about it so very often, long before she'd attempted her first dungeon play party and met Ethen.

Though she tried to shut him out of her mind, something must have shown on her face.

"What were you thinking?" Marcus asked, leaning sideways as he set her empty bowl aside and checked her hands behind her back.

"Nothing, Sir." Not wanting anything to stop this yet, especially not something as inconsequential as blocked circulation —she'd regularly suffered far worse than numb fingers in Ethen's play scenes—she stiffened her spine. Pushing her shoulders back, she locked her hands so the edges of the cuffs weren't quite so cutting, but Marcus had already stopped. Propped as far back as his chair would allow, he studied her with a flat, unsmiling mouth.

"You want me to believe you had that look on your face with absolutely no thought in your head? Did you just lie to me, Anna, or were you thinking about him?"

Pony flinched, not knowing how to answer in a way that wouldn't automatically ruin both their fun. No dom wanted to be mentally compared to another. No dom wanted to be lied to, either.

"Were you thinking of him?"

She flinched, unable to hold his steady gaze. The tension in her own throat was choking her, she couldn't swallow much less speak. She nodded, knowing that would be punished.

"Thank you for the truth. I expect you'll be thinking of him for quite some time. Next time, just say so."

Her mouth dropped. "Y-you... you're not angry?"

"Do you want me to be?"

Definitely not.

She was still trying to figure out how to answer when he ordered her to stand.

She'd taken too long to answer. Now he'd be angry with her. Now she was going to be punished.

She stood up, relief that it was finally going to happen helping to balance her instinctive dismay at her inability to keep anyone happy.

He got up too and disappeared back down the hall. A few minutes later, he returned with a partially full black duffel bag. The contents made a heavy, clinking-clattering sound when he set it on the end of the table. The look he gave her when he unzipped it sent shivers dancing through her already rattled nerves.

He went through the contents, pulling out two neatly bound lengths of black bondage rope. "I know you like this, so these will be used."

He put them on the table by his bag, then dug down into it again. He pulled out a medium-sized paddle. A good eighteen inches long and half an inch thick, she knew by experience how sharp and stinging that would be with every impact. She tried not to show any response, but relief tickled her none-theless when he discarded it in favor of a smaller leather paddle. He set that on the table, then added a black and blue colored flogger with twenty or more two-foot-long falls, a stainless steel butt plug, nipple clamps, and lastly a vibrating wand.

"I'm going to go clean your floor. You," he said, beckoning her close enough for him to remove her cuffs, "will clean the kitchen. Afterward, I want you to choose among these things, which you'd like to be rewarded with."

She tried not to react, but she couldn't stop staring. Raw electric need was humming under her skin right alongside stark, naked fear. He said reward, but she'd made a lot of mistakes tonight. Just being here with him was deserving of anything but a reward, and yet at no other point since she'd met him had Marcus done anything except exactly what he'd said he would.

Choose?

She looked at her options, utterly baffled because she didn't know him well enough to guess what he wanted to do to her. Five options. That gave her a one in five chance of selecting the right thing, and four in five of screwing up. The stress of it knotted instantly.

"Just...Just one, Sir?"

"Pick as many as you want," he said. "The only requirement is that you choose things *you* want to do. If you're not comfortable with me using one of these items, then put it back in the bag. If you want to spend the night tied up, I'm fine with that. If you'd rather I not shove this up your ass"—he picked up the butt plug—"then put it in the bag, because if it's still on the table I'm taking that as consent and shoving it up your ass." He promptly exchanged the plug for the wand. "If you don't want me to send you to bed tonight with explicit instructions to make yourself come, then put this back. If I find out later that you weren't honest about this and submitted to something that left you feeling violated because you're trying to give me what I want, I'm going to be beyond pissed off. I mean it, Anna. I want to know *what you like*. Got it?"

"B-but what if what I want is to give you what you want?"

He came around the table at her, and it took everything she had to stay where she was. To neither retreat nor flinch as he took a looming stance over her.

"You want to play that game?" he softly countered. "Then prove to me you know how to give consent and, more importantly, how to take it away when you need to. You're absolutely no good to any dom if you can't be trusted to play safely."

"Yes, Sir."

He left her standing at the table, staring at options. Her stomach rolled until she felt sick. She had no idea how she was going to choose. She knew what she liked, but that held little merit when compared to what he liked. She'd rather take a hundred hard strokes of that medium-length wooden paddle than to find she'd chosen something he'd find boring. She didn't want to be boring. She didn't want him to give her pleasure when he himself received little to nothing in return.

She backed from the table.

She hated spanking, but if he enjoyed it, she'd much rather give him the pleasure of reddening her ass than just about anything else.

Did Marcus want to play with her sexually? She hadn't had anyone touch her like that in over a year. And yes, she was Master Ethen's property, but he was dead. He'd also shot her, so really, why did he get to continue having a say?

She didn't like pain, but she'd had her breasts tormented with a zip line once and even lightly caned and that had been kind of fun.

She wasn't a huge fan of anal when it was being done to hurt, but she had liked it the few times Master had done it gently. She'd liked being told she was Master's dirty little cum slut. Just not when he was passing her around among his friends.

And the wand? She hadn't been allowed to masturbate in years, not since she'd first met Ethen. How was she supposed to make herself come when she could only ever achieve orgasm when Ethen gave the command?

This was impossible. She couldn't do this.

Retreating into the kitchen, she put the food away, washed and dried the dishes, and tried to figure out where in which cupboards each one's 'proper place' was. By the time she had nothing else to do but confront once more her impossible choice, she felt sick enough to want to throw up again.

Somewhere down the hall, Marcus was steam-cleaning the rug. She could hear the vacuum humming, and it gave her hope that she still had time to agonize her way through to a decision right up until the vacuum stopped.

Then she panicked.

She was failing. He was going to be so angry.

This was so stupid! Why couldn't she just pick something? Why wouldn't her shaking hand move?

Down the hall, the vacuum started up again and the relief buckled her knees. She collapsed on the floor in front of her waiting selection while the shame of her indecision reduced her to tears.

Covering her face with both hands, she tried to stem back the tide, but once one got out, they all got out. The snap came from deep inside her when she broke and the pain at first was so crippling that she couldn't even stay on her knees. She keened, the weight of her sobs pushing her so far forward that her face touched the floor.

Useless.

Stupid.

Better off dead.

Self-pity gave way in a rush of hot fury. Fury because she'd given how many years to that man and look at her! Look at what she'd become.

Pathetic.

Hopeless.

She covered her head with both arms, feeling every tear at her soul as she fell apart as quietly as she knew how. The running vacuum down the hall would cover some of the noise, but she knew better than to get caught. And she had already cried so much.

A warm hand settled on her back between her shoulders, another taking her by the arm and pulling her up off her knees. It took him two tries, her body just wouldn't cooperate, and the dismay at hearing that lie of a vacuum still going while Marcus bent to hook his strong arm around her waist, physically picking her up off her knees even when her legs refused to obey, was just as cutting as her sadness.

"I'm sorry," she wept.

He pulled her into his arms and, without a word, held her while she cried.

She tried so hard to stop, for his sake. No dom wanted to watch a woman cry, unless of course he was actively in a mood to wring the tears from her. Ethen loved tears. Usually, he'd been aroused by them, but even he had his limits and a Menagerie girl knew better than to cry, ever, unless they were in a scene. "It can always be worse," as he was so fond of saying, usually when he'd caught one of them breaking this unspoken rule, and usually when he was showing in exquisite detail just how much worse he could make it for girls who interrupted his peace of mind.

"I'm sorry," she whispered again, struggling to get it under control.

Folding his arms that much tighter around her, Marcus rocked her. "I'm sorry too," he finally replied. "It was a test, honey. You're going to get a lot of them. But how else are we to know where to mend, if we don't first discover the places he broke. It's okay." He rubbed her back. "You did exactly what I thought you'd do."

A test, and she'd failed it. Obviously. Miserably.

She crumbled in his arms, burying her face into his soft shirt and letting it absorb the last of her tears. She must have found her limit of them, finally. They stopped altogether then. She waited, feeling the heat of him, breathing in the faint spice of whatever deodorant he used, her hands limp at her sides, for him to let her go now. But he didn't.

Stroking her hair back from her face, his hand brushed the softest caress down her back from her shoulders to her waist.

Her breath caught, a tiny hitch no different from all the hiccups she'd gasped into his chest between sobs. Except this one was different. Nothing had changed. She'd still failed his test; she'd failed a lot of things today, this week... this year. And yet he was touching her, touching her hair, her shoulders, caressing his hands down her arms from the balls of her shoulders to her wrists, caressing her hands, even her fingertips.

Her breath caught again, her fingers erupting into tingles as he so lightly stroked every part of them—fingers, thumbs, the backs of her hands, her palms. Like he was reading her like a blind man read braille, holding her so close to him, unable to use his eyes and so he was using touch.

It was strange.

It was heaven.

A part of her itched to step back, to keep this from becoming stranger still while she figured out what he was trying to do. But that errant part was overridden by the rest of her, all the other parts that were coming alive in now flashes and champagne sparkles as his warm, rough hands moved back up her arms to her shoulders. He started all over again, shifting that starting point to her back. Laying his palms flat, he caressed straight down her back, sweeping over her shoulder blades, down her ribs, to her waist.

Her nipples pebbled. She didn't mean for them to, it just happened, and he was holding her so close that if she didn't move away now, he would soon begin to feel them, brushing against him as she breathed.

Move...

She didn't. Moving risked him stopping this... whatever *this* was and she couldn't.

So she stood there, tiny shivers raking her as he reached her waist. Pausing, he let his hands rest on her hips, lightly massaging, before again up his hands came, settling once more on her back, just off her spine now. Down they caressed, and the shivers grew in intensity. Nerves she didn't know she had anymore were all coming sharply back to life. All were rejoicing. All were aching for him to touch them next.

Her right knee tried to buckle, but she stiffened her legs, fighting the weakness as his hands came back to settle on her shoulders.

"It'll be okay," he said, the head of his fingertips following the nape of her neck up into her hair. He alternated, stroking and massaging her scalp, weakening her all over again. "Say it with me, Anna."

"It'll be okay," she whispered, adding her quivering voice to his stronger one. He touched her ears, smoothed his thumbs down over her cheeks, the heat of his breath breathing life into the cold void that had been living in her so long she was barely aware of it anymore. She felt it now, only via the contrast of the warmth of his touches.

"It will get better," he said, drawing back just far enough to touch his forehead to hers. "Say it."

"It will get better." She trembled, heat unfurling in her belly, in her breasts, in her face where he was touching and between her legs. Heat upon heat, upon throbbing aching heat licking through the furrow of her sex until it reached her clit. He didn't caress her there, but he touched her face, letting his braille-reading hands follow the line of her jaw, the bow of her lips, the curves of her narrow cheeks, even the bridge of her nose.

She could have cried when he slowly let her go and stepped back.

He took her hand, she looked down at it, watching as if it were happening to someone else as he started down the hall, gently drawing on her lightly imprisoned fingers until she stumbled into step behind him.

He was taking her to her bedroom.

The heat in her clit became an eager pulse. Her nipples were tight as beads and the soft shirt she wore now felt as course as burlap everywhere that natural movement made it brush and tease her breasts.

He was going to take her. Electrified need shivered through her pussy, jolting all the way up to her womb.

She wasn't so desperate as to think he wanted her, but he was a man and she was a woman. More, he was a dom and she a submissive. All he had to do was want something and she was here. For more of these touches, she would happily give him anything he desired.

It had been so, so long...

Her knees were shaking by the time they reached her door. He pushed it open, revealing the vacuum, noisily running next to the closet where he'd put it after cleaning up the mess she'd made. The room smelled faintly of lavender and soap. He took her to the vacuum first, turning it off before leading her to stand at the bedside.

Her knees almost buckled again. How would he want her? On her knees, serving him with her hands and her mouth... hers was watering already. Would he lay her on her back on the bed, or turn her around and bend her over it? Was he even erect, she didn't dare bring herself to look and though her fingers twitched to touch him, she wasn't brave enough to do that, either.

Letting go of her hand, he drew the bedcovers and motioned her to get in.

She looked at the sliver of waiting mattress as he held up the blankets, waiting.

Tiny twitches of disappointment cut between the heated pulses still throbbing hopefully between her legs, but she crawled into bed. She lay on her back, not at all under-standing when he covered her over and tucked her in.

"If you need to get up in the night to get a drink or visit the bathroom, you may. I want you to sleep, so you may not watch television. If you want to masturbate, you may.

Morning comes early in this house, you'll want to be well-rested." He touched her again, his hand settling briefly on her head once he was done. "Good night, Anna. I know you don't agree, but you did well tonight."

He left, switching out the light on his way out the door. He left the door cracked and then he was gone.

She lay between crisp cool sheets, every inch of her awakened and wanting, rejected and denied.

She'd done well?

Was this another test, would he come back? Maybe he was giving her time to get used to the idea of servicing him. How many times had he said he wasn't her dom, after all?

Was this her punishment for failing the last test?

Rolling onto her side, Pony curled into a ball, but though this would have been the time for it, the tears didn't come.

A few minutes later, the light in the hall winked off and she heard the soft bump of another door closing. She stared through the darkness in her new room, her body more alive than she could remember it ever having been, but he didn't come back. He'd gone to bed.

Disappointment cut like a razor.

Welcome to her new life.

Marcus

MARCUS LAY on his back in bed, staring through the darkness at a ceiling he couldn't see. One door down the hall, Pony was lying in bed, her little nipples tight as beads, that slow flush of unmistakable arousal staining her cheeks. Though he'd given her permission, she wasn't masturbating.

He hadn't really expected it. Orgasm control was one of those things a lot of doms enjoyed doing to their subs. When done right, it was a fantastic and pleasurable experience for two people in a committed relationship. Few thought about what would happen later on, when the relationship failed and suddenly the sub lost access to the command she'd trained herself to obey so completely that she could no longer disobey it, no matter how much she wanted to.

Pony didn't want to, but he'd seen just how much she'd liked being touched as he'd consoled her.

Consoled. He felt like an ass. He hadn't meant to turn her on... at first. He'd deliberately left the vacuum running so she wouldn't suspect he was creeping down the hall to check on her. When she'd broke down, he couldn't stop himself.

She'd been alone and unhappy for so long. Comfort, that's what he'd told himself he was doing. But then, he'd seen how she'd responded—the quickening of her breaths, the slight arching of her back as she'd tried to prevent him from feeling the tiny points of her nipples brushing against him.

How long had it been since she'd had the pleasure of gentle human contact? He'd given it to her, telling himself with every soft caress of his hands that he was doing this only to be kind.

He wasn't kind. It had been a long time since last he'd touched anyone too, though he had only himself to blame for that. The consequence of it came rushing over him halfway through the second slow stroke of his hands moving down her back. It would have been so, so easy for him not just to touch her face, but to tilt her mouth up and he knew she wouldn't have resisted if he'd kissed her. She might even have wanted it. That she might not want it, but might do it anyway just so she could serve him was the only thing that kept him from crossing that line.

She'd felt good in his arms, though. She'd felt better than

good; she flicked every one of his triggers—vulnerable, so he could be strong, submissive, so he could take charge.

He shouldn't be thinking about this. He definitely shouldn't be thinking about her as if they were at a club and she were begging for a scene. This was a job.

Oh, who was he kidding? He hadn't deprogramed anyone in years, and it showed. Everything he'd done with her so far he'd done wrong. He knew better than this. He knew better than to get emotionally involved with the person he was trying to help. He had to stay hard. He had to stay objective. Few people could imagine the daily hell of living under the cultish leadership of another. Ethen O'Dowell wasn't a religious or government-defying extremist, but he absolutely qualified as a monster for the level of control that he'd exerted over his 'menagerie.'

Was she masturbating yet?

Marcus turned his head. On the table by his bedside, the baby monitor relayed quiet proof that she wasn't. She might not know how anymore. He couldn't exactly show her, but regaining control over her own sexuality would have to be part of her program. She needed to be able to live again, on her own. She needed to be strong enough not to fall victim to the next asshole wannabe 'dom' she met once she passed the court's requirements and he no longer needed to worry that she'd end up in a hospital psyche ward.

Step one: She had to be able to take care of herself.

Step two: She had to be able to make decisions. He'd worry about smart decisions later, right now, he'd be happy just to see her break free of Ethen's programing enough to make any kind of decision on her own.

There were other steps, lots of little landmarks that he knew in his head, if she could just reach them, would mean she'd stand a better chance of never becoming another person's mindless victim again.

But she was so damaged, and it had been so long since he'd done this kind of work. She might be better off with someone who was fresh. Someone still in the business, who'd maybe studied psychology and who had a degree to help him unravel the mental roadblocks that Ethen had successfully erected inside his 'pony.'

There might even be someone out there who could do all that and who was kink-friendly.

Someone with two legs and who wasn't every bit as damaged as Anna was, albeit in different ways.

He'd made so many mistakes with her tonight. He'd give up her care in a heartbeat if only he could think of someone capable of taking over for him and who he'd trust not to make the damage worse.

He couldn't think of anybody. If forced to be brutally honest with himself, he wasn't sure he'd have released her anyway and he couldn't say exactly why he felt so conflicted about it.

He lay there well into the night, listening to the sleeplessness of the woman in the room just down the hall. Knowing he'd done just about everything wrong today that he could have; knowing he needed to change his approach if there was going to be any hope of success tomorrow. He knew how he wanted to change things, but that would be walking such a dangerous, temptation-laden path.

The stump of his leg ached in dull throbs of relief now that it was free of its prosthetic. The dull throb of his cock bothered him more, and it only got worse as he considered in his head all the things he could be doing—but never would—with the submissive down the hall.

CHAPTER 5

Pony/Anna

He wasn't kidding last night when he'd said six o'clock would come early. It hardly felt as if she'd slept before Marcus knocked once on her door before cracking it far enough to call, "Out of bed. We've got things to do."

He didn't come inside. He didn't even linger in the doorway long enough to see if she obeyed. By the time she'd pushed the blankets aside and sat up on the edge of the bed, he was gone and she was alone.

For the first few minutes the foreignness of the room was almost impossible for her to get past. It wasn't that she'd magically forgotten the last few days—the hospital... Ethen... Marcus's guardianship—but as she rolled to sit up on the edge of a bed that wasn't hers, for those first few unguarded moments, she actually looked across a room that was so obviously not Puppy's, fully expecting to see her in her childhood bed complete with its My Little Pony bedspread and Back-street Boys poster on the wall. Then she saw the scale, and the paper tacked to the wall, and the lingering dampness of the carpet beneath her bare feet, and gradually she reoriented to her new reality.

It was the second day of the rest of her life without a master.

Shoulders slumping, she got up.

"Five minutes," Marcus called as she wandered down the hall into the bathroom. "Consult your list and get your butt in gear."

Head bowed, Pony closed the bathroom door and did what she needed to. Her feet dragged. Instead of washing her hands, she stood staring at herself in the mirror, her gaze wandering over the shaved side of her head while the water ran down the sink. She'd once had such pretty hair. She used to get compliments on it every time she went to the salon; she used to love the stares when they'd gone to the club. She knew how beautiful she could be, all decked out in her harness and her Pony gear, her naked breasts on display, her hair drawn up in a long ponytail mane that ran all the way down her back, the wisping tips just brushing the swells of her ass. Men had wanted her. Women had wanted her too, and envied her.

She reached up to touch the metal staples she couldn't see, tracing the ridged ladder of them holding the back of her scalp closed. It was tender, and the headache was still there. She supposed she ought to be grateful she didn't look worse.

Wilting, she left the bathroom. As she wandered back down the hall to her room, Marcus didn't shout anything further at her. She glanced over her shoulder before she went into her bedroom, but she couldn't see him in what parts of the kitchen or living room could be glimpsed beyond the end of the hall.

She was pretty sure her five-minute grace period was up,

but she couldn't seem to gather the will to hurry. Closing the door behind her, she took off her shirt and climbed onto the scale. She stared listlessly as the arm thunked in acknowledgement of a little weight gained. All that cheese in last night's supper, she supposed. She reached up twice to adjust the weighted balances, but she stopped both times without touching it. She got off the scale without recording her weight, got the too-big sweatpants out of the closet and put them on.

Marcus was standing at the kitchen sink in black sweats and a grey tank top that showed off every hard knot of muscle that bunched and relaxed as he drank his coffee.

"What time is it?" he asked as she came as far as the kitchen table and then stopped. The black duffel bag and all those selections from last night were gone. Laying in its place was a long, heavy paddle. A good two feet in length, the thick business end was wider than her hand was flat, and a braid of red and black leather wrapped the handle in a sturdy grip.

Her wary eyes snapped from it to him, but her stomach already knew what that was there for. Instead of knotting in dread, it blossomed, swirls of that same blessed heat that had so tormented her when he'd touched her last night reigniting as if it had never stopped. Her butt knew better. It cringed, a far more practical response.

"Don't," he warned, his gaze fixed on her over the rim of his cup, "make me repeat myself. You will not like how I do it."

Swallowing hard, she looked to the clock on the stove. "Six-twenty-one," she forced herself to admit through a throat gone suddenly quite dry and tight.

"Remember your list from last night? We agreed that you had from six to when to get ready?"

Her breasts rose and fell in swift, shallow breaths. "Six-fifteen."

"It stands to reason that six-fifteen should be what that clock says then, in order for you to be on time, doesn't it?"

"Yes." Her stomach was swirling, her thighs clenching. Liquid heat was trickling down between her legs, drawn to the erotic pulse of a clit gone crazy. She didn't even like spanking. She didn't like pain.

"Did I give you a five-minute warning?" he continued, setting his coffee cup down on the counter.

Her throat was tightening, but her pussy thrilled as he came towards her. "Yes."

Marcus stopped directly in front of her, within easy reach of that paddle. "What's your safeword?"

She was breathing too fast and yet it she could hardly feel herself getting the air she needed. "Red, club rules."

He picked up the paddle. "Bend over. Hands on your knees and you'd best brace yourself, because you're going to need it."

The look he gave her as he walked around behind her released a heated flow of wetness that spilled through her pussy lips in a mortifying rush that was as unexpected as it was crazy.

Pony looked at the floor.

"You either safeword," he ordered, "or you get your ass in position. Right now, or I start adding strokes."

She bent over. Widening her stance, she propped her shaking hands on equally shaky knees and did her best to brace herself. The swirling heat and gushing wetness only got worse as he sentenced her.

"Six strokes, one for each minute you were late. Two more for the deliberate disrespect you showed me. Count them."

There was almost no time at all between the end of his brief lecture and the fall of that first mighty swat. It cracked into the seat of her sweats, catching both bottom cheeks dead center, almost knocking her off her feet and jolting her all the way up on tiptoes. Pony shouted, grabbing the backs of her

75

knees to keep from clapping her hands on her wildly smarting ass.

She immediately got back into position, her wide eyes staring desperately at the floor. Her shaky breath nearly choked her as she struggled to keep her voice menagerie girl calm as she dutifully said, "One, Sir."

It hurt. Oh, it hurt.

He swung the paddle again, landing the second swat every bit as hard as before and in the exact same place.

Although better prepared for the impact, Pony still bounded up. This time she did grab her ass, rubbing fiercely with both hands and bouncing in place.

She was appalled at herself, even as she begged him, "W-wait, please wait!"

Tapping the paddle impatiently against his leg, Marcus stared back at her, utterly without sympathy. "That's two. You've got six more. Want to start over from the beginning?"

Her clit rejoiced at the severity, but her clit was crazy. Her ass stung furiously, igniting into the worst kind of fire. The sort that hurt so much she could barely stand to be in her own skin.

He arched an eyebrow. "Safeword?"

She turned around. In took every ounce of courage she possessed, but she bent down, cringingly offering her ass for the next stroke.

"Three, Sir!" she shouted as the paddle whacked sharply— that same damn spot—throwing 'hurt' into a realm of bonfire pain she couldn't remember ever suffering the likes of before. The next crack took the fire even higher and it was everything she had not to jump up again. "Four, Sir! God!"

"Is this what you were looking for this morning, when you made the decision to disrespect me and my time in my own house?" Marcus asked.

"No, Sir!" she cried, her voice shaking every bit as badly as her legs.

The crack of the paddle was merciless. She broke down, sobbing, shoving hard on her knees to keep from dropping to the floor. It was the only place she could go, because if she stood up again, they'd start over.

"Count," he reminded.

"Five, Sir!" she wept, tears pouring from her. Heat scalding her. Her pussy throbbing in time with the furious pain eating her up alive.

Six walloped her, knocking her half a step forward. She made herself get back into position. Why, oh why had she taken so long in the bathroom?

"Count," he sternly reminded a second time.

"Six! Six, Sir, please!"

The seventh was merciless, striking exactly where the other six had already bitten in. Her flesh was throbbing, scalded, hurting more than any spanking Ethen had ever given. Mostly because, he never gave spankings. He'd beaten, whipped and caned, and every time he'd done it, he'd done so to satisfy himself. He'd never bothered to lecture. Never in all the years she'd been with him.

She bawled. "Seven, Sir!"

The eighth and last stroke hewed into her, hard, but no harder than any of the strokes that had come before it. She barely kept from collapsing to the floor. She had to grab the backs of her knees again to keep from grabbing her bottom.

"Eight, Sir!" She wept, grateful that it was over and sorry to the depths of her soul for whatever broken thing inside her had made her disobey him in the first place. She hung her head, sobbing and waiting, determined to hold her position until he gave her permission to rise.

He didn't. Instead, in the same stern lecturing voice, Marcus said, "Did you weigh this morning?"

Scrubbing the back of her hand across her cheeks, she wiped away her tears. "Yes, Sir."

"Were you up, down or the same?"

"Up, Sir."

"Did you record it?"

She stared at the floor, her breath catching in hitches and hiccups. "N-no, Sir."

"Why not?"

Because she hadn't wanted to. She stared at the floor.

"Bare your ass."

She burst into tears all over again. She also didn't bother standing. Hooking her thumbs in the waist of her sweatpants, she pushed them down. The elastic scraped over the swells of her already raw and sore ass.

One more, that was all he gave her, but on bare, fiery flesh, the crack of the paddle was deafening and the sharpness of the pain so blinding that for a moment, all she could do was bawl. She held herself in position, barely, dreading the more that she was so sure would follow until she heard the faint clatter of the paddle being laid back down on the table. He took hold of her pants, pulling them back up over her deep red bottom.

"Go record your weight, wash your face, and be back here in two minutes. I don't like starting my day late."

As he headed past her into the kitchen to get his coffee, his hand fell on the top of her hair. He stroked her, the only sign of forgiveness he offered, but it worked.

Pony rose, her bottom on the most painful fire, but every step she took back to her bedroom felt somehow lighter. Gone was that depressing weight that had consumed her when first she'd awakened this morning. Her hand was shaking as she recorded her weight. Her face was red and her eyes watery and swollen, but she felt so much better as she bent over the bathroom sink to obediently wash her face.

She was well within her two-minute deadline when she returned to the kitchen. Whoever would have thought a spanking could actually make her feel better instead of worse?

~

Marcus

HE'D DONE EXACTLY what he'd said all day yesterday that he wouldn't do. He'd treated her as if he were her dom and she were his to command.

Hip propped against the kitchen sink, his coffee in his hand, Marcus crossed his ankles and waited to see how she would emerge. Had he just made things better or worse?

With roughly thirty seconds left until she hit her deadline, Anna came back down the hallway and he got his answer. She wasn't smiling, but her step was lighter, her back straighter, her shoulders no longer hunched as if she were a shell of a woman going through the motions, but thrown back. Even her eyes looked clear, not haunted or sullen, or even sad.

He'd got it right.

Pushing off the sink, he got a bottle of water from the fridge and handed it to her. "Had you been on time, I'd have let you have coffee. Now you'll have to wait for breakfast. Sad, that you'll have to do your exercises with a hot ass. Still, the choice was yours. Follow me."

Water bottle in hand, she trailed him through the kitchen as obediently as a well-trained puppy.

The basement stairs were concealed behind a door near the entrance to the garage. He hit the light switch just inside and headed down the plain wooden steps. Of all the rooms in his house and barn included, this was the one Marcus spent most of his time in. This was his home gym and the biggest reason he was able to walk now as well as he did, without a cane despite the bullet fragments still lodged in his hip and his below-the-knee prosthetic. As far as he was concerned, everything he needed was right here. A mat in the middle of the floor where he could do his yoga, two treadmills up against the wall from when his ex-fiancé and submissive had lived with him, the well-used punching bag on which he regularly beat his frustrations, and in the corner, the weights that kept him toned. Solid body, solid mind—even temper, that had become his motive shortly after his failed attempt to eat a bullet.

Megan hadn't enjoyed this room as much as he had, but she'd tolerated it. Mostly because he hadn't given her a choice. He didn't intend to give Anna one either. She came down as far as the bottommost step, and then he heard her footsteps stop when she paused to look around. The floor was cement, the ceiling bare wood rafters with three hanging lightbulbs evenly spaced in sockets down the length of the room. The tiny utility room at the end was where the furnace, water heater and a narrow set of supply shelves kept his gym from looking too dungeon-esque. In that regard, he supposed, the spanking bench, St. Andrews' cross and padded horse in the corner probably didn't help. Unlike the exercise equipment, those articles hadn't seen any use since he'd told Megan she needed to find someone else. Someone whole. A dom worth following.

Yeah, his depression after his injuries hadn't been kind. Not to either of them.

Crossing the floor to the supply closet, he dug out Megan's old yoga mat, something he'd been more than tempted to toss out on a number of occasions. He was glad he hadn't now.

Dragging it back with him, he dropped it on the floor a

short distance from his mat, toed it into an even position with his own, and then snapped his fingers and pointed at it.

"Front and center," he said. "Let's get to work. You ever tried yoga?"

Pony came to him, shaking her head. When he pointed again, she stepped onto the mat.

"I'll teach you, we're going to do this every morning."

Working out with someone else wasn't his favorite experience, never had been. Exercise had become his retreat. He loved to make it burn, to push himself harder and farther, until the sweat was pouring off him and by the end he was just sitting on the floor, too fucking exhausted to move. Since his accident, that had become to him what sex and topping used to be. It had to, deprived of the latter by his broken body, he'd needed something to pour his energy into while he'd struggled to climb out of the self-pity wallow he'd built for himself.

It was easy to see now that wallow had been the reason he and Megan broke up. At the time, he'd thought he was being sensible, but he'd pushed her away. The more she'd said she loved him, the more she'd cried and tried to hold on to what they had, the more he'd been convinced he couldn't give her what she needed. He'd worn her down until she finally gave up and left.

Water under the bridge. She was married now to some guy she'd met at Black Light. More than that, she was pregnant with their first. Which, he supposed, just went to show how things had a way of turning out.

As he began to show Pony her new warmup routine, Marcus was prepared to feel that same old sense of irritation at having his alone-time invaded by another. Right from the start, though, this felt different. Pony offered no complaint and she needed very little instruction beyond a few posture corrections as she tried to copy him through his stretching exercises. She was quiet, she paid attention. She was flexible as hell too, and that was a pleasant surprise which in retrospect probably shouldn't have been. Her Dom had been a jackass. Of course, he'd want his slave to be flexible when he wanted and fit.

"You have a morning routine?" he asked, watching as she straightened and spread her legs, then bent down with him to press first her hands and then her elbows to the floor. That was impressive. He had no problem getting his hands palms flat without feeling more than the pleasant pull of his leg muscles relaxing in the stretch, but Pony was damn near folding herself in half.

"Not for a while," she confessed. "But we used to exercise every morning and every day at noon."

"Your choice or his?" Like he had any room to judge Ethen on this level.

"We had a scale in our house too," she said, rising back to her feet as he did.

She didn't elaborate. He connected the dots without needing her to.

"Again," he said. "Was that your choice or his?"

"His," she said softly.

They moved into the next position.

"What was your required weight?" he asked, almost certain it was going to piss him off to hear it.

"One hundred five."

Yeah. He had no problem judging the man on that one.

"You realize I'm not going to give a shit what the scale says. I'm going to make you gain until you start looking healthy. After that, it's up to you if you want to gain more. But there will be no dropping under the healthy mark, not under my roof. Got it?"

She folded herself when he did, bending into another low stretch, and didn't say anything.

Having her here beside him didn't irritate him, but not being answered did.

He pulled out of the stretch, crossed onto her mat, grabbed the front of her shirt and pulled her all the way up until she was nose to nose with him.

"I asked you a question."

Her face was every bit as blank as it had been in the hospital. The only thing missing from it then was all that misplaced anger he'd since watch her exorcise. She looked perfectly calm now, perfectly... defiant in a very quiet, non-confrontational way. One had to look very closely to see the glitter of that defiance in the depths of her too-blue eyes as she studied him.

"When does it become mine to control?" she finally said.

"What?" he countered. "Your body or your weight?"

"Both."

Oh... good girl. Annoyed as he was, that she would stand up to him on this was almost a reason for pride. "Depends. Do you like being a human skeleton?"

"Not particularly."

"So long as you're healthy, I won't have a problem with your weight."

"So long as I'm not losing weight."

"That's right."

She hiked her chin. "And when I start tipping the scale in the other direction? What are you going to do then?"

Now he really was proud of her.

"So long as you're healthy," he repeated, "I don't care what you weigh. If you're waiting for me to say the punishments'll come out, you'll be waiting a very long time. I don't work that way."

When she didn't argue, he moved back onto his mat. Catching his left ankle, he moved into the next position. She did too, although she wasn't as steady as he was as he stretched.

"That's the way you were this morning," she finally got brave enough to point out.

"You were testing me and you know it."

They switched positions twice more before she found the courage to argue again. "You said you weren't going to do that. You said—"

"I'm not your dom," he finished for her. Yeah, he was still trying to figure that out for himself. He shouldn't have paddled her. He'd never meant to let anything between them come close to any kind of topping relationship. That that was the last thing someone as badly damaged as she needed had been foremost in his mind right from the moment he'd decided to go get her, bring her back here, try to help her. That it might be exactly what she needed had been the thought he'd gone to bed with last night and when he'd put the paddle on the table this morning.

"You said you wouldn't," she said again, no trace of petulance or accusation anywhere in her words.

"I changed my mind. You want to do real yoga now, or hit the treadmill?"

"Why?" she asked, and he didn't for a second thing she was talking about exercise.

Dropping his non-prosthetic foot, Marcus walked back onto her mat, getting nose to nose with her again. He wasn't trying to threaten her. He didn't want her to feel intimidated. He probably shouldn't have done it at all, except it felt more intimate this way.

"Because you needed it," he told her. "Are you trying to tell me you didn't, because if that's the case, I'll happily wash your mouth out for lying."

She didn't. Her chest rose and fell in short, shallow breaths, just a little faster than normal and not because she was winded from the stretching they'd done. "I'm not saying that."

"What are you saying?" he softly challenged, trying to gauge if she was scared. "That you didn't like it?"

She wasn't quite fast enough to shutter against the confusion that ever so faintly wrinkled her brow, before vanishing again. She was good at hiding what she felt. Survival 101. That was what happened when one lived with an unpredictable abuser.

"I didn't like it," she said. That shadow of bewilderment that briefly disrupted her careful mask made him believe she probably wasn't trying to lie. "I don't like pain. I'm not a masochist."

"You don't have to be a masochist to like it when someone takes charge of you. Whether you physically liked the sensation of being spanked or not, you did like that I held you accountable. I told you what to do, you didn't do it, and I executed the consequences. That was what you liked. Would you like me to prove it?"

She was trying to control the shallow swiftness of her breathing, but there was no hiding that telltale flutter of her pulse, beating in the hollow of her slender neck, marred by bruises from last night's botching suicide attempt.

She wanted to chicken out, he could tell by her eyes. She shifted on her feet. It surprised him that she didn't back away.

"How?" she asked.

"Put your hand in your pants," he told her. He'd had her bent over in front of him with her legs widely spread and her pants down around her thighs. He knew what she was going to find, whether she wanted him to or not. "Touch your pussy."

That fluttering pulse beat wildly beneath her pale skin. Her face remained a mask. "Why?"

"Because," he answered, smooth as silk. "When you show me your fingers afterward, they're going to be wet as hell."

Her nostrils flared, her eyebrows twitching once, the

corner of her mouth quickly following suit. What was that expression? Was she scared, embarrassed? Aroused? It pricked at his pride that he couldn't read her. He only just controlled the instinct to take hold of the waist of her too big sweats, drag her right up to him until they were belly to belly, and hold her gaze steady with his while he reached down between her legs and checked for himself.

That would definitely be crossing a line.

Like this wasn't?

He both saw and heard her swallow.

"Did you masturbate last night?" he asked, already knowing she hadn't. Lying awake in his own deprived hell, he'd listened to all her most subtle movements and the only thing he'd heard all night was her tossing and turning.

She only half shook her head before she froze again, a little bird in the paws of a very big cat. He wasn't trying to stalk her, but he couldn't make himself stop. He couldn't even say he was trying to help her anymore. "When was the last time?"

"We're not allowed to do that. Menagerie girls are for him. Our pleasure is for him and only when he—"

"Yeah, I get it." It was too important that he let her talk about her abuser for him to bristle like this when she did, but he didn't want to hear about that asshat. He wanted to hear about her letting her fingers do the walking, letting her body arch and writhe to the practiced caress of her own fingertips. Did she like soft petting? Did she go in hard and fast? Did she like to sink her fingers as deeply into her sweet pussy as she could reach, trying to satisfy that inner aching need that could only truly be satisfied by the eager thrusts of a man's cock? "Do you come when he commands it?"

Her nipples had tightened under her t-shirt. They were little points now, thrusting out to meet him. His fingers itched to touch them, but Marcus kept them firmly at his sides.

"Yes." She couldn't quite make herself nod.

"When was the last time he told you to come?"

A brief glimpse, that was all he caught of the raw dismay that shattered her mask, right before she swallowed, looked away, and found another hard mask. This one was cool, almost haughty. Despite the watery shine slowly seeping into her eyes.

"I don't remember. A month before his arrest. Maybe two." She folded her arms across her breasts. "He didn't want me himself. He gave me to his friends. H-he made me come for them."

Not want her? Marcus barely kept from saying Ethen was an idiot and a fool, as well as an asshat. God, he wasn't supposed to want her and it was everything he could do right now not to take hold of her wrists, pry them off her chest, and tell her never to hide her reactions from him again. He wanted to see them. He wanted to feel them in a way that had absolutely nothing to do with helping her overcome the hell she'd been through so she could once more face the world without fear.

He was supposed to listen when she talked of Ethen. Encourage her to share her feelings without disparaging the man, because her loyalties to him at this point would make her clam up fast and it would only be that much longer and take that much more effort for him to get her to open up again.

He was supposed to listen.

But right now, the only thing he was listening to were the layers of hurt exposed in tiny twitches beneath her breaking mask and the throbbing ache of his own heated arousal.

"I don't want you to come for them," he surprised them both by saying. As if he had the right, as if she should even care. As if it weren't dangerous for him to give her a reason to care. "But I do want you to come. Does that scare you, piss you off, or excite you?"

He didn't need to ask. That fluttering pulse of hers leapt so hard when he'd said it that he could have seen it from space. His cock twitched in response, tensing, tightening, stirring within the confines of his own sweats. All she had to do was look down and she'd notice something no professional in his line of work would ever let himself become in the presence of a client.

"I-I—" she stopped and stared at him.

She didn't know what she was feeling. Fair enough.

"Touch your pussy," he ordered.

Her arms unfolded just a little too fast to be compliance. Her hands dropped to her sides while the tight peaks of her nipples tented the front of her shirt. His mouth watered, but he kept his eyes squarely locked with hers.

"Now," he said. A dull throb of anticipation built low in his abdomen as his cock hardened.

She swallowed again, but she still didn't back away. She was too well-trained for that, and that both pleased him and pissed him off.

Hesitantly, she slipped her hand into her too-big sweats. Her cheeks colored as she watched him, that beautiful flush making her even more lovely to watch as she pushed her arm down between her legs. He knew by the flinch of her stomach when she touched herself. His cock twitched too, sending that tiny shock of excitement racing through his veins.

She stared at him, frozen with her hand between her thighs.

"Show me," he said thickly. It was his turn to swallow now. He ached to see the wetness glistening on her fingertips. He hungered for it.

Reluctantly, she drew out her hand and there it was, fingers just as wet as feminine arousal could make them. Her hand trembled as they both looked at it.

Good girl. The praise never quite made it from his mind to

his hungry lips. He nodded instead. He made himself back away. If he didn't, he didn't know what he'd do. Take hold of her wrist to bring those delectable fingers to his mouth so he could explore her taste. Cup the back of her neck, dragging her to him for his first kiss in what had been way too long for him.

Obviously, it had been way too long for them both.

It would be wrong, no matter what he did. He was already in the wrong. She was doing this of her own volition, but he was in charge here and she was damaged. He was taking advantage of his position over her. He was taking advantage of her inability to consent to the measure of control he was exerting.

He shouldn't want her this powerfully.

That he did was as shocking to him as it was dismaying. He'd never, ever done this to any other woman he'd taken under his protective wing. He was not showing himself to be worthy of her fragile trust.

He took another step back. "Twenty minutes on the treadmill," he told her. "Nothing above a brisk walk. I need to go upstairs a minute."

Turning on his heel, he made himself leave the basement in slow, measured, unconcerned steps, knowing it would only do more damage if her submissive mind jumped to the conclusion that she'd disappointed him somehow, that the wetness on her fingers or her obedience in revealing it had turned him off.

Off was nowhere near what he'd been turned, and if he didn't get space between them right now, the urge to completely violate the authority that he'd been given over her was going to get the best of him.

He went to the kitchen and made sure she could hear every one of his steps loud and clear as he got a water from the fridge, popped the top off at the sink and made himself drink it. He ought to get an ice cube and apply it where the cold could only help the most, but that just made him think of the last time he'd indulged in ice play and how Anna might respond if he splayed her out on her back, tying her legs wide apart so he could torment her clit with piece after wet, icy piece. First her clit, then her folds, and then he'd fuck her with it, slipping as many watery cubes up inside her as he could make fit, letting them melt while he then turned his attention to the bud of her little asshole and, with another piece of ice, made her scream while he fucked her.

Would she scream? He'd bet she was too well-trained for that. He was just as certain of his own skills and, given enough pieces of ice, he knew he could break through that training and leave her writhing, squealing, maybe even sobbing long before he fed her his cock and rode her mouth, her cunt or her ass until he'd exhausted himself. He didn't care how cold her flesh, he'd warm it.

"Jesus," he muttered, shaking his head at himself. Drinking the rest of the water bottle was a poor substitute for what he really wanted—Anna, lying on her back, with the playground of her body laid bare for him to conquer.

CHAPTER 6

Pony/Anna

*B*reakfast was two eggs, bacon, toast, orange juice and coffee. Fresh from her shower, it was impossibly hard for Pony to sit at the table and watch while he cooked it. She was supposed to do the cooking. Not because she was good at it, or because she liked it—she didn't particularly, although she had felt pride on the rare occasions when Ethen had compliment one of her meals—but because he was serving her. It should have been the other way around.

Also, the chair was devilishly hard and although the worst of the heat and throb from her paddling had long since faded, sitting on this unforgiving seat briefly rekindled the burn and just made the lingering tenderness hurt.

"Can I help?" she asked.

His back to her while he worked at the stove, Marcus calmly replied, "While I think it's fabulous that you feel comfortable enough with me to even make that offer, what did I tell you the last time you asked?"

Oh yeah. She had already asked. She'd forgotten.

Menagerie girls weren't supposed to fidget, but she had to get the nervousness out somehow and though she did try to still it, her fingers stubbornly picked and picked at the cloth of her sweatpants. She wasn't any good at being waited on. She hated the uselessness. She wanted to *do* something.

Looking for something to clean, she spotted the blanket he'd swaddled her on the couch with last night still lying where she'd left it. It was literally the only thing she could see out of place in the whole of his house, and she stood to fetch and fold it.

"Sit your butt back down," he said without turning around.

"But I was—"

He set down the plastic spatula he'd been using to scramble the eggs and plucked a wooden spoon from the utensil crock by the stove. He turned around, but she had already shut her mouth.

Still calm, without a trace of irritation or anger, he said, "You're not the world's slave, and when you leave here, I don't want you hooking up with the first asshole you meet. That means you need to learn when to serve and when to sit while other people do things for you."

Right. She eyed the wooden spoon and prayed he'd be content with just lecturing her.

He waited, and when she didn't argue, he put the spoon down on the counter and went back to his eggs. Releasing the anxious breath she'd been holding, Pony squirmed, but stopped almost immediately. Her butt was too sore to wiggle about. How did brats do it? *Why* would they do it? There was absolutely no appeal to the dull ache that her inadvertent writhing had rekindled in the deep muscle of her flesh. And yet, there was no denying that the look he'd given her while he'd wordlessly threatened her with the spoon had sent another hot rush of arousal spilling down through her core to soak into her pants.

She touched her stomach, pressing down as if she could still the fluttery spasms twitching through her sex, but it wasn't her stomach where she wanted most to be touched. And it certainly wasn't her hand that she wanted most to feel.

She pressed harder, catching her forehead in her palm as she braced her elbow on the table and tried not to ignite in another heat wave of mortification. He'd had her touch herself. Right there in front of him, and though he'd walked away immediately afterward, she'd known he'd liked what he'd seen. He'd liked how wet he'd made her.

She did too.

She knotted her fingers in the excess folds of her shirt, locking them in place so she wouldn't be tempted to reach down and do it again. Menagerie girls weren't for themselves. Their bodies, their pleasure, their pain—all of it belonged to Ethen. He decided what, where, when, and how. In the beginning, she'd really liked that. She'd liked walking with him in the park, in broad daylight, never knowing if the mood would strike him and he'd pull her off the path far enough to be out of sight, before backing her up against a tree or bending her over behind a bush and making his use of her.

She'd liked the ecstasy of his whispered command, 'Come' burning in her ear.

She'd even liked the unbearable erotic frustration if he chose to finish before her, leaving her perched on that razor's edge of unfulfilled passion without allowing her release.

But this... this had been different. Marcus had wanted her. At least, he'd seemed to, and even though he'd walked away, he'd done so leaving no doubt anywhere in her mind that her obedience had pleased him.

She'd liked that.

The whole time on the treadmill she'd been able to think about nothing except the tented glimpse she'd caught in his pants as he'd gone upstairs and what she might have been allowed to do if only he hadn't left just then. What she would have done had he asked her to ease his hunger instead. Or maybe, had he asked her to masturbate for him, like he had last night. She'd have done it, right in front of him if he'd wanted her to. For a moment, just thinking about it, she felt beautiful.

She rubbed her stomach, feeling again that blossom of heat slowly building while her pussy fluttered its wanton little spasms.

Her breakfast plate came into abrupt view, startling her as Marcus set it on the table in front of her. He set a fork down next to it, and then sat down at the head of the table beside her.

"Eat," he said.

A man of many words he was not, but she didn't mind.

Untangling her fingers from her shirt, she dutifully picked up her fork and began to eat.

"How long were you with him?" he asked, putting egg on his piece of toast before taking a bite of both.

The mention of Ethen startled her again, but not in a good way. She didn't want to think about Ethen right now. "Four years," she said, swallowing a twinge of guilt for thinking that along with her first sip of hot coffee.

"You like it black?" He gestured to her coffee. "I've got cream and sugar if you prefer."

Another flush of heat hit her, warming her belly in a way that had nothing to do with the coffee wending its way through her. "I'd like that, yes, please."

Ethen liked his coffee black, so all the Menagerie girls had their coffee black. Even after he'd gone to prison, she'd continued to drink it that way, even though she much preferred the bitterness softened and sweetened.

"Good girl," he said as he got up.

She startled. "For what?"

"For stating a preference."

"Wh-what do I get for getting up and getting it myself?" she offered, because watching him do it for her was killing her.

He brought the wooden spoon back to the table with him, along with both the sugar and the cream. He didn't say anything. He didn't have to. The threat was there in the way he placed it between their plates.

"Okay," he said, picking up his fork again. "Now you ask me something."

Startled all over again, she snatched her gaze off the spoon. "What do you want me to ask?"

"Dealer's choice. It's called conversation and it's something most people enjoy while they're eating. Especially if they're sharing company."

Her mind went completely blank for all of two seconds, before a slew of completely terrifying questions popped into it. She didn't dare give voice to any of them. What if they were too personal? What if she was asking the wrong things? She tried to find something that didn't have anything to do with whether or not he'd wanted to have sex with her downstairs. Something safe.

"I'm not asking you to bring me the moon," he drawled. "I'm asking you to get to know me."

"What if I ask the wrong thing?"

"No such thing." He took another bite of egg, and chewed it all while giving her a knowing look. "Also, that didn't qualify as a question. Ask me another."

She flushed and cast about the table as if some saving hail

Mary question might pop up there for her to borrow from. "Um... W-why did you come to the hospital?"

"For you," he said evenly. "Spencer called me up, said there was someone who needed help. That was before you got shot, by the way. A good week before. Did you know that?"

"Spencer doesn't like me," she said, not at all sure why he would have called anyone much less Marcus on her account.

"He liked you well enough to call in a favor. Your turn." Finishing off his first piece of toast, Marcus brushed his fingers over his plate and then pointed to hers. "Also, conversation doesn't mean you get to stop eating."

"My turn?"

"Yeah, we're doing this in turns. You asked me why I came for you, I answered. Then I asked you did you know. You answered, it's your turn again."

"I asked you my turn and you answered that," she pointed out, her stomach tightening as she waited to see if she'd just irritated him.

He stopped mid chew, then looked at her. A very reluctant smile tugged at his mouth. "Clever. You got me."

He wasn't mad. His slow chuckle made her want to smile too, but this was all so new and she didn't know if a back-handed slap might still be coming.

Picking up another piece of toast, he scooped egg onto it as he thought. "If I'd made blueberry pancakes in the shape of Mickey Mouse, would you eat it with syrup or whipped cream and sprinkles?"

"What?" Taken aback, now she laughed.

"You need to answer me first, or I'm not accepting your question." He was still smiling, though, and the unexpected silliness of what he'd asked threw her.

"I, um..." She didn't know how to answer. How ever he served it, that's how she'd have eaten it. She tried to gauge if he was a whipped cream and sprinkles kind of guy. To be honest, he didn't look like a Mickey Mouse pancake person, either. "Syrup... I guess?"

"Because you like syrup, because you don't think whipped cream and sprinkles qualify as breakfast foods, or because you think that's what I like?"

"All of the above," she decided. "Why would you ask me that?"

"I'm gauging whether or not you might be a Little."

Her jaw could have hit the table. "A-are you a Daddy Dom?"

"Nope, but one thing you learn once you've been in the lifestyle long enough. You never say never. I could see myself playing the part, for the right submissive." He winked at her over a bite of bacon. "And you'd look great in pigtails. Just saying."

She was so startled, she laughed out loud. She quickly clapped a hand over her mouth to stop the sound, but one look at his face told her that while he might currently be teasing her, he was also serious. That made her laugh all over again. He thought she'd look good in pigtails? Shock and delight battled until it was all she could do to stay sitting in her chair. Her nerves were tingling. She didn't want to leave, but she ached for movement.

"Have you ever had a dom put your hair into pigtails?"

She shook her head. "No, I've only ever served. Really, I've only ever dreamed about doing serving."

Was that sad or just pathetic? She sat, staring at her half-empty plate. It felt like a lifetime ago that she'd first ventured into Black Light, first scened, first met Ethen and fell in love with his absolute dominance. Fell in love with him.

She'd been so young back then. She felt so very old right now.

Old and tired. Her smile faded as she stared at her plate.

"You're not eating," Marcus reminded. "It's also your turn."

She picked up her fork again and poked at her eggs. He'd broken the ice, been the first to ask her lifestyle questions, so she gathered her courage and took a chance on irritating him with one of her own. "Have you got a submissive?"

"Used to," he said without hesitation. "Her name's Megan. We were together for, oh... five years or so." Eyebrows arching to show the seriousness of the relationship, he said, "I almost married her."

She really was prying now, but her next question was out before she could stop herself. And it wasn't even her turn. "Why didn't you?"

Shifting in his seat, he picked at his toast. "Because I was stupid," he finally admitted. "A job went bad and I got hurt. Lost my leg and of course, I picked up all the baggage that comes with suddenly finding yourself to be literally half the man you were. You know, that sort of bullshit."

She shook her head. "Half the man?"

"You know," he said again, but she didn't and her look must have said that for her. Both sighing and chuckling now, a self-depreciating sound, he spelled it out for her. "I wasn't good enough anymore. I couldn't walk, I couldn't stand, I couldn't fuck her. And no," he added wryly when she blinked. "There's nothing wrong with the equipment. But the phantom pain was constant back then, and you try getting into the mood or holding onto an erection when your leg's in agony all the time. I wasn't taking care of her needs; she was taking care of me twenty-four-seven. I knew she had to be miserable, though she denied it. But I was stubborn, and I just knew she had to be. So, eventually I wore her down until she was miserable, then I told her to go. Finally, she did."

"You loved her," Pony said softly. It wasn't a question and he didn't have to answer. She could tell just by looking at him. He'd loved her a lot.

Marcus picked at his toast for almost a full minute in silence. "Very much," he agreed with a nod. "But, sometimes things work out for the best even when it feels god awful and wrong all at the same time. Megan's happier now, and she's definitely been happier with the guy she's got now than I would have made her since I lost my leg." He looked at her. "You may not have noticed, but I'm not always smiles and sunshine."

Despite the sad turn the topic had taken, that vastly under-stated comment made her laugh again.

"Looking back on it all," he softly asked, still picking at his toast, "do you think you loved your master?"

That he was able to say the word without sounding as if he were mocking Ethen or her was the only reason she answered him instead of immediately shutting down.

"Yes, but not... not in a love-love kind of way. I mean," she huffed, trying to bring back the laughter although she wasn't feeling it anymore. "He was everything I wanted a dom to be, at first. He was my first real experience and he gave me every-thing I thought I desired. He hit every trigger, was attentive and dominant. The sex was fantastic." She took a bite so she would have a reason to stop talking, but the taste of it was gone and all she had was dry ash in her mouth by the time she swallowed.

"You sign a contract?" Marcus asked.

She nodded. "Twice," she said, half laughing at herself. "First when we played, and then again when I moved in." She thought about it. "Three times, actually. I signed another when he decided he wanted Kitty."

"She a Menagerie girl too?"

She nodded. "His second." She glanced up from her plate long enough to flash him a wry smile. "His favorite. And then, within a year he found Puppy. She was more of a whipping post, though, really. He... was really bad to her, and Piggy. She was the last one and the first to break free. It's all her fault that things fell apart."

Except it wasn't, and looking back on that night, Pony couldn't imagine what it must have been like for Piggy. She couldn't imagine how cold it had been, being made to kneel naked in that mud wallow, and for what? For daring to tell him that she wasn't happy and didn't want to stay. Her 'defiance', her 'disrespect' had set Ethen off for hours. He'd ranted and paced the house while Piggy had been outside, kneeling in filth.

Filth had been her special punishment, because it hadn't taken Ethen any time at all to realize how OCD Piggy was about keeping herself and everything around her clean and tidy. Especially her hands. She was always washing her hands, and within days of taking her into his Menagerie, Ethen found something to punish her for just so he could march her out to the pig pen that hadn't seen use in all the time that Pony had been on his farm. He'd wet it down in preparation for her. He'd been throwing food scraps out into it for days, prior to her 'infraction,' something so small that Pony couldn't remember even what it was. He'd made Piggy kneel in it because it was the one thing above all others that she couldn't stand to endure.

Just like the box under Ethen's bed had been the one thing that claustrophobic Kitty could barely tolerate, and yet that was how he'd punished her. He'd make her crawl on the floor, sleep in the kitchen, use the litterbox, eat and drink from food dishes on the floor—if he was mildly annoyed. When he really wanted to punish her, he put her in the box, turned out the lights, and waited until she broke down past sobbing, begging, kicking and clawing to get out. Past screaming—those had been awful nights. He'd wait until she was practically cata-tonic before he'd let her out. Sometimes it took days for him to be satisfied.

Puppy had her kennel, her beatings, and her ostracization. Ethen barely let her belong in the first place. She was always on the bottom of the pecking order and they all had treated her that way. Even after he'd gone to prison and they'd have nothing left but each other, Pony had clung to Puppy, but she had ordered her about too. Kept her in line. Bullied her.

Slapped her.

Pony looked at her food. The only one who didn't have a special punishment was her.

Except, that wasn't quite true, she thought with a suddenly pang of hurt. The only thing Pony had wanted more than anything was for Ethen to love her. And practically from the beginning, what had he done but bring other women into the home he'd allowed her to share. Ethen's home, yes, but she'd lived there with him. At his request... his command.

Kitty, Puppy, Piggy... with each one he brought home, she'd put on a fake smile and pretended it was fine, but deep inside it had felt as if he were cutting her into pieces. He'd called it a poly household, but really, he was just replacing her without releasing her. And she'd spent four years convincing herself it was fine, because for as long as she accepted it, she could be with him.

She'd convinced herself it was fine if he wanted to share her with his friends, too. She belonged to him, heart, body and soul, and if it brought him pleasure to watch other men fuck her, then she was happy to do it. Except that, it hadn't brought *her* pleasure and she'd been far from happy. But he was the Master and she the submissive, and any attempt to talk to him about it was viewed as sedition. Then, instead of loving her, he'd punish her—refusing to look at her, talk to her, command her. He'd banished her from his bed and, when he was really annoyed, he'd forced her to put on her full Pony gear, tie her over the horse in her room, and whip her with the crop until she would do anything, promise anything, just to get him to stop.

Yes, Ethen was good at finding punishments that, rather than fitting the crime, fit each submissive's worst fear and greatest insecurity.

Right from the beginning, he'd identified hers, and she'd loved him for it.

Pushing back his chair, Marcus reached over and took the fork from her hand. Her breakfast began to blur when he took her wrist next, pulling gently until she finally had no choice but to get up.

She wasn't going to cry. She refused to cry. For God's sake, she'd cried a fucking river in the last few days. She was done. And yet, when he drew her down to sit on his lap, her shoulders started shaking and out the tears came anyway.

"I'm so stupid," she wailed, offering no resistance as he pressed her head down onto his broad shoulder. His arms folded around her, embracing her tightly. "He really hurt me, and still, I miss him."

Marcus said nothing. Rubbing her back, he rocked her instead.

She wasn't worth comforting.

She shoved to get off his lap, but he refused to let her go. A flash of anger cut through her and she lashed out, punching his shoulder. One blow was all it took for every thread of self-control she had to simply snap. She wrenched to get off his lap, but he locked her down, holding her while she kicked and beat and finally just screamed.

As fast as it hit her, the rage was gone, leaving behind only the worthless realization that Ethen had never really wanted her. He'd never loved her, never desired her, never enjoyed her in any regard except in the pleasure he found in depriving her of everything, including her self-respect.

"The heart's a wretched thing," Marcus said simply, once

the worst of the storm had passed and only her unending river of tears remained.

And maybe that was the saddest part of all. Here they were, sitting over unfinished breakfasts and each missing someone they used to love, but which a bullet beyond their control had robbed them of.

"Life sucks," she hiccupped between sniffles.

"Sometimes," he agreed. "If you think this is going to get you out of finishing your breakfast, however, I've got a paddle that says otherwise and no problem taking your pants off while I use it."

He was rocking and cuddling her, so Mr. Hardass he wasn't, but it struck her as funny. Laughing through her tears, this time when she pushed to get off his lap, he let her go. Returning to her own chair, she gingerly lowered herself to sit, picked up her fork and, with a sigh, ate the damn eggs.

CHAPTER 7

Pony/Anna

"I can't do this," she said, gripping the envelope with the money he'd given her in both hands.

"Yes, you can," he replied, like this was no big deal at all, but she knew better and she was serious. She couldn't do this. She knew she couldn't because he wasn't the first person since Ethen had gone to prison to try to send her shopping. Puppy's mother had done it too, and then called her useless when she'd had a meltdown in the bread aisle. How did one even begin to find the right loaf when the list just said 'bread' and there were a dozen brands, a million varieties, and she had no clue what everyone liked?

And *this*, what he wanted her to do first? *This* was going to be even harder.

Bowing over in the passenger seat, Pony did her best to put her head between her knees, the way he'd taught her yesterday when she'd had a meltdown over which cup to use when she made her morning coffee. The man had a twenty-mug collection of all colors, shapes and humorous sayings. Ethen had had three coffee mugs, all exactly the same and no menagerie girl was allowed to use them.

"It's a test, but an easy one," Marcus had told her, arms folded across his chest, hip propped against the kitchen island, ankles lazily crossed while he watched her agonize in frozen indecision. "Out in the real world, honey, no one is going to care which mug you use. Take a deep breath, reach up your hand, and pick one."

Easy to say, but what if she got the wrong mug? What if she picked his favorite, or picked one with sentimental value? What if she dropped and broke it?

"Any mug," Marcus had coaxed her, and it took ten minutes and actual tears for her to finally put her hand on one and pull it down. "Now, put coffee in it and take a sip." He waited while she obeyed. "See? The world didn't end."

No, but the effort had exhausted her and she ended up wanting to go back to bed instead of drinking coffee.

Now they were doing the dressing debacle.

"Can't I go back to Puppy's and just get my own clothes?" she begged, but from the driver's seat, already Marcus was shaking his head.

"I already told you, honey. I sent Spencer to get them before we left the hospital. Cynthia's mom threw everything out. Nothing of yours was left in that house."

Sitting side by side in his vehicle, they stared through the windshield at the busy Goodwill. She felt sick.

"Can't you do it?" she begged him. "Please, just this one time?"

"I can." He nodded, then swung his head to pin her with the same stern look that over the last week she had both come to love and hate. It was a look that said he'd happily give her what she wanted, but she wasn't going to like how he did it. "In this case, however, I really think you should do this yourself."

"Why?" she cried, but she already knew.

Normal people didn't have meltdowns in the morning when it came time to dress themselves. Normal people didn't stand agonizing in front of their closet, staring at the options —of which hers currently consisted of four pairs of sweat-pants and six of Marcus's cast-off t-shirts—practically in tears because she didn't know what he wanted her to wear. Followed quickly by 'Ethen would never let her wear any of this.' Half the time she'd cry, but eventually she'd pull some-thing out and put it on. And she hated every minute of it.

Every fucking thought in her head went through that 'what would Ethen think' cycle first and she couldn't stop it. Marcus didn't care what she wore; he cared that she went through the process and put something clean on every morning instead of simply wearing the same articles she'd stripped off the night before. He'd only let her get away with that the first morning, then he pulled several tubs out of the attic and expanded her wardrobe by those extra sweatpants and t-shirts, and even added a flannel nightgown meant for someone a good eight inches shorter than she was. She had yet to wear it.

"Why can't you just be a nudist?" she muttered, rubbing her face with both hands.

He snorted and laughed. "You can do this."

Yeah. She could do this. He said that just about every morning while she went through one of her mini meltdowns. Meltdowns because she had to pick her own clothes, melt-downs because she then had to dress herself—and frankly, she'd been struggling to do that for weeks now, all the way back when her relationship with Puppy began to fall apart and she could no longer depend on her sub-mate to be there to help her. The difference there was that those had been her clothes. They were familiar, and had already passed the 'Would Ethen let her wear that' quandary. She'd gone through them diligently, breaking everything she owned down into two categories—work clothes and home clothes, and the only reason that had worked was because, like Ethen's coffee mugs, they were all almost exactly the same.

Shifting behind the steering wheel, Marcus checked his watch. He didn't even try to do it subtly.

"You ready to go in yet?"

God, no. She shifted now too, and tried again to put her head between her knees. The dashboard got in the way, so she rested against it instead.

"Okay, head back on the seat," he said.

She did, moaning, "Can we go home yet?"

"Do you have two full sets of cloths and dinner for tonight in the backseat?" he countered.

She couldn't even get herself out of the car and he didn't need a vocalized answer.

"Then we're not going home. Close your eyes."

Breathing out, she did. After a week with the man, she'd become as familiar with his relaxing exercises as she had his tests.

"You're sitting on a beach," he began. "The sun is warm on your shoulders, and the breeze that's blowing is just enough to keep it from being too hot. It pulls and plays with your hair."

She had to force herself to picture the beach instead of the store, and the first thing she thought of pulling and playing with her hair wasn't the breeze. It was the way Marcus took hold of her hair and marched her into the bathroom this morning, forcing her to stare at herself in the bathroom mirror and take back the self-depreciating comment she'd made. She barely remembered what she'd said, but she remembered the fierceness of his stare in the glass as he'd scolded her.

She remembered the pressure in her scalp, too, as he hauled her right up onto her tiptoes and then yanked her pants down, letting them fall all the way to her ankles. She remembered the stab of wanton anticipation that went straight to her pussy as he'd whipped the hem of her shirt all the way up to his hand in her hair, holding it not only well up out of the way, but all the way up to her neck, effectively stripping her naked.

She remembered he'd said, "Five things. I want to hear you say five nice things about yourself, right now."

She remembered being completely unable to come up with anything at first and that, mad as he'd been, he'd been the one to come up with the first thing.

"You have beautiful eyes."

She'd looked at herself in the mirror, staring into her own eyes almost surprised.

"Say it," he'd ordered, and promptly brought his open hand smacking down hard across her ass once she had.

He'd made her come up with four more on her own.

"I used to like my hair" hadn't counted, but the last one that she'd come up with had. "I'm a great service submissive," she'd told him, her ass stinging every bit as fiercely as her eyes as she held his stare, daring him to disagree. He hadn't. He hadn't disagreed with any of the silly things she claimed to like about herself. Her eyes... okay, they really were kind of pretty and she liked that he'd noticed. Her hair... okay, that probably really hadn't counted, since she wasn't saying she liked it, but that she used to like it. The others... that she made good coffee, that she had nice feet, that she liked her ponytail... those were just bullshit. The coffee maker made good coffee, feet were ugly no matter who they were on, and the only thing she really liked about her ponytail was Marcus's propensity to grab hold of it when he wanted to make sure he one-hundred-percent had her undivided attention. And he did, every time. Her body came alive when he did this—lectured her, pinned her in the ferocity of his authoritative stare, and especially when he spanked her, the flat of his hand measuring swats like a baker measured teaspoons of spice and flavor extracts.

"I'm a great service submissive," she'd said, and he hadn't disagreed. For a moment, he didn't swat her either. He'd held her stare in the mirror, holding her yanked up onto her tiptoes by her ponytail, and he didn't say anything at all, but she didn't need him to. She was too mesmerized by all the things he wasn't saying. The darkness in his stare grew subtly darker still. He'd tipped his head. And then, instead of swatting her, he'd smacked his hand down between her legs, grabbing hold of her pussy to yank her hips back from the sink, and the next thing she knew, she was bent flat over it.

He'd spanked her then, hard, swift swats that had continued to fall until the sting turned to smart, the smart to hurt, the hurt to fire and she lost all ability to hold still or take it quietly.

She did take it, though. Whether she liked spankings or not hadn't mattered, it was what she could get and she accepted it for what it was—a good substitute for what she'd wanted from the moment he'd grabbed her pussy. As if he'd owned it.

And he kept right on spanking her, long after the point needed to be made. She could tell by the way he held her stare in the mirror, he did it not because spanking her was what he wanted to do, but because it was what he could trust himself to do.

"Are you even listening to me?" Marcus asked, snapping her back to where she was, eyes closed in the passenger side of his car.

"On a beach," she said, heat flushing her every bit as hot as if she were baking in the sun. She squirmed, the warmth of embarrassment nothing compared to the wicked burn thumping and throbbing between her legs. She clenched her thighs, but her clit would not be muted.

"Uh huh." He didn't sound convinced, but he didn't rub her nose in it either. "You're comfortable, relaxed. Walking along the water's edge, the wet sand warm beneath your bare feet."

"Am I naked?" She relaxed, liking the image he was conjuring. She hadn't been to a beach since she was a kid. It had been a fun day, right up until she got stung by a jellyfish.

Clearing his throat, Marcus said, "You are not." His normally calm and soothing tone had changed. It was now terse, almost abrupt. "You're wearing a bathing suit. A one-piece," he decided. "With a sarong. So no one can see your red, welted ass except me."

"You're there?" she asked, a little surprised. He'd never put himself in one of these meditative relaxation scenarios before.

"No," he said, hints of annoyance creeping into his tone. "Yes, maybe. But no one else. You're supposed to be walking on the beach alone."

"I don't mind if you're there." She'd have preferred it, in fact. "I hate being alone. Where are you?"

"Walking right behind you."

She'd have much preferred to have him walking ahead of her, so she could follow submissively in his footsteps. Then it hit her. "So you can see my ass and no one else can?"

"You know what—get out of the car, go in that store, and buy some damn clothes."

His minor distraction worked or at least, she didn't feel

sick to her stomach as she shouldered open the door and got out. He got out too.

"Money," he reminded.

She'd left it in the car. She had to go back, digging between the cupholders and the seat until she found the envelope with the three crisp twenties that Marcus had given her. She couldn't remember the last time she'd handled money with the intent of spending it on herself, when she didn't have an outlined plan given to her by her Dom.

"Just two outfits," Marcus said, waiting at the hood of the car for her to come back to him. He continued waiting too, his knowing eyes locked on her until, shoulders slumping, she took the uncomfortable lead and walked into the store ahead of him.

Two outfits. That was all she had to do, but the second-hand store was huge. From the front doors, there were three checkout registers to her left, and from the right all the way into the back of the store where the furniture was being displayed, were row after row after row of overflowing clothing racks. Children's were in the middle of the store, just behind a display of higher quality purses and costume jewelry. Men's were past the registers, on the far left.

Overwhelmingly, most of the clothing was women's, starting with pants, then skirts, then shirts and dresses. They even had nightgowns.

"You can do this," Marcus told her. "One step in front of the other. Just imagine you can feel that warm, wet sand between your toes."

There was no sand. There was no beach. She really was going to be sick.

He nudged her back, trying to get her walking, but there was a woman in the shirt aisle looking her up and down, her expression screwed up in that same look she'd received so often, especially in those last months at Black Light when everyone hated her.

She'd have turned and walked right back out of the store but for Marcus, and the warm clap of his hand on the back of her neck. He didn't care who was looking their way, he marched her into the pants aisle, turned her to face the clothes, gave an extra squeeze of warning to the back of her neck and then let go.

Pony closed her eyes, struggled to take a breath, and then knowing it would send her spiraling harder—maybe even because she knew it would spiral her—she glanced at the woman again. The woman had gone back to her shopping.

Pony stole quick glances around, her gaze flitting from shopper to shopper, but no one was looking at her anymore. No one cared that she was in the store.

Her silent shadow, Marcus folded his arms across his chest and waited for her to do something.

Two outfits, she told herself, her nervous hands alternately rubbing and crinkling the envelope with the money he'd given her. Because this was her test. Not only did she have to pick out her own clothes, but she was going to have to go shopping for dinner and show that she could buy food for herself without having a meltdown in the grocery store.

She was ready to have a meltdown here.

Clothes.

"Break it down," Marcus told her softly. "Break it down if it's overwhelming, and just focus on one thing at a time. What do you put on first when you get dressed?"

She looked at the pants in front of her. It was all jeans. Nothing but jeans, a veritable rainbow of denim in every color from white to black. Skinny jeans. Low riding jeans. Ripped jeans. Jeans with fancy stitches and rhinestone butter-flies on the pockets.

She could practically feel Ethen's slap to the back of her head for even looking at them.

She squared her shoulders. Turning on her heel, legs shaking, she walked the entire length of that and the next aisle over. She found the skirts, but they didn't have a lot in her size.

"You prefer dresses?" Marcus asked, trailing along behind her.

Ethen had preferred dresses. It was a requirement that he be allowed access to his property whenever and wherever, and pants restricted that. So did underwear. Toward the end, he hadn't even allowed them clothes at home. There were days he took them out into public completely naked except for their harnesses and knee-length coats.

She pretended to sort through the sparse selection, but all she could think about was walks in the park in nothing but a coat, in the kind of weather that made coats really obvious, knowing people were watching them, hearing again Ethen's whisper telling her who to approach and when to flash.

"That one... that man's been watching you since we got here. Go. Ask him if he'd like to fuck you in the bushes."

Her knees ready to buckle, she turned from the skirts and walked on, her hands shaking, her stomach knotting. The selection of dresses was slightly better than the skirts, but most were ten years out of date or completely inappropriate to everyday living. Matronly and maiden styles were all mixed together. The submissive in her wept and could cheerfully have convinced her to get lost in sorting them out into their own sections, but it was a stalling technique and she knew it. She didn't want to touch these clothes, much less sort them. She just wanted to quiet that seductive voice in the back of her head that kept bringing up memories she wished she could forget.

This was ridiculous. She had to pick something.

Blowing out a shaky breath, she grabbed a hanger, pulling it off the rack and looked at the yellow summer dress. It had flowers on it. Flowers, for God's sake.

She hung it back up. Black. That's what she needed, just plain black with a white top. Something professional. Something that wouldn't make her look ten years older or worse, younger than she was. Something that wouldn't look like she was trying to pick anybody up.

Five minutes, that was what Ethen would say if he was standing here. *You've got five minutes to take someone back into one of those dressing rooms. Don't make me punish you.*

She hung the dress back up, but her hand was shaking so badly it fell off the hanger into a puddle on the floor.

Pick that shit up, Ethen hissed.

She dropped, grabbed it, shoved it back on its hanger.

"Anna, why are you shaking?"

She snapped around, fighting herself to keep her face blank and her breathing slow and steady.

That guy in the corner is watching you... he wants you...

The only man she saw in here beside Marcus had to be seventy if he was a day. He had a cane and an oxygen tank, and he was standing by an equally elderly woman in the furniture section, looking at lamps.

You've got five minutes... I want you to blow him in the dressing room...

"Anna?"

Her skin was crawling. She took off walking again, her back straight, her knees threatening to give out at every step, but she got out of reach before Marcus could do something like put his hand on her shoulder. She didn't want to feel him touching her, not right now. Not with Ethen's voice hissing in the back of her head as if he were standing right here with her. He'd never set foot in a thrift shop, not in all the years she'd known him. He always took her to the mall when he wanted to humiliate her like this. She couldn't count the number of men she'd blown in those dressing rooms.

Fingers grazed her elbow, but as she reached the end of the aisle, she broke into a run. She tore past the jeans and was out the front door so fast that the store clerks probably thought she'd stolen something. She hadn't. She buckled over on the sidewalk almost as fast as she reached it. Grabbing her shaky knees, she sucked for air that was coming too fast and yet wasn't enough. Her ribs ached, her heart pounded so hard. If everyone wasn't staring at her before, they were now. The sidewalk of the thrift shop strip mall was not empty of passengers and when she straightened, grabbing her head and then her heart, everywhere she looked, people were all she could see.

One guy who had been heading the other way when she'd come bursting out onto the sidewalk turned around, like he intended to come back to her, and Pony panicked. She bolted for Marcus's car.

She fumbled with the locked door, her panicking fingers unable to figure out why it wouldn't open before the car chirped and suddenly it did. She dove into the front seat and quickly slammed and locked the door. Her back was straight, her head was high, her badly shaking hands were palms flat upon her thighs, and she couldn't breathe. No matter how fast her chest was rising and falling, she couldn't get any air inside her.

Marcus was coming out of the store now. There was no judgment on his face. Only quiet acceptance, as if he'd expected her to meltdown and be unable to do it.

Of course, he had. She hadn't been able to do anything yet without freaking out at least once. She couldn't shower and wash her own damn hair. She couldn't put herself to bed without being told. She couldn't sit on the furniture, or fix something to eat or drink anything but water without permission. She couldn't use the last of something, or make a mess, or leave behind anything that might show she even existed.

She couldn't hold a job anymore. She didn't have money of her own anymore. She couldn't go in a fucking store and pick out a stupid dress without hearing that man's voice whispering commands she'd once lived in dread of hearing.

And now here came Marcus, his car keys in his hand and his face set to take her home.

Fury blasted through her, every bit as cutting as the panic had been. Shouldering the door open, she jumped out and slammed the door again. Storming past him, she went back into the store. People were definitely staring now. She cared, just not enough to stop.

She went straight to the jeans and grabbed two. One had rips and the other more sequins than an a-list movie star at the Grammys. She took it to the checkout counter. There was no line, but the clerk looked at her as if she were holding a gun instead of pants.

"Having a good day?" she asked cautiously as Pony dumped her purchases on the counter for her to ring up. Where was her money? Her hands were empty. Even knowing they wouldn't be there, she looked under the pants and then spun around, in an absolute panic. She'd dropped it! Where had she dropped it?

The distant thump of a car door shutting barely caught her attention, but the sight of Marcus coming back into the store with her envelope held up so she could see it did. She wilted, her relief fast fading into depression as he came into the store to rescue her at the checkout. Because she just couldn't do this by herself.

"Nope," he said, when she tried to sidestep so he could take over. He handed her the envelope. "You've got this. You're doing fine."

He was a liar. She was anything but fine. She was practically in tears.

Still, she paid for the jeans with one of the twenties, waited until she was given her change and then quietly followed him back to the car. She folded herself into the front seat far more quietly than she had the last time. Knees drawn up to her chest, she hugged her purchase and herself, making herself as small as she could. She'd never felt quite so incompetent in her life.

"Okay, that was a good first run," Marcus said as he got into the car next to her.

It wasn't funny, but she laughed at him anyway.

"Let me see your purchases."

Depressed, she showed him each pair, draping one after the other over the dash, first the one with ripped legs and then the sparkling ones. She let him get a good look.

"When was the last time you wore jeans?" he asked.

She heaved a sigh. "I can't remember."

"Your choice, or his?"

His. It was always his. She didn't answer, but she supposed that was an answer in and of itself. She picked at a rhinestone.

Marcus was far more practical. He picked up the first pair and checked the size. "Size four, huh? We'll have to put some weight on you before they fit, but they'll be a closer match than Megan's old sweats."

She looked at him. "I... I'm wearing your ex's clothes."

"Some. Some are mine. I bought them for her, so I guess she left them here. She wasn't much of an exercise bunny to start with. She only worked out in the basement because I told her to. And after I got hurt, I really threw myself into the workouts and I... really made sure she felt shut out of it while I was down there." A corner of his mouth curled up in a self-deprecating smile. "It's really hard to do your best and still know you're failing, especially when there's an audience."

The depression died. So did the last fading remnants of panic and anger, so tightly intertwined that she couldn't feel anything beneath the tidal wave of hurt now trying so hard to drown her. She didn't want to cry. She was so tired of crying. She swiped at the tears before they could do more than build along her lashes, stole a quick gasp through her mouth, and then nodded. "Yes, it is."

"Whose voice did you hear the strongest in there, mine or his?"

She laughed again. It still wasn't funny. Shaking her head, she looked out the side window so he wouldn't see her face. She didn't want him to know.

"Are you hearing my voice now?" he calmly asked.

She nodded.

"Look at me."

She didn't want to, but menagerie girls did as they were told, and she'd been the first and the best of them for so long, she didn't know how not to obey. She met his steady gaze.

"You," he said, slow and serious, "did great your first time. This wasn't easy. I never said it would be. But you still did it, and you did it very well."

"I'm pretty sure I'm a size zero," she said, tiredly.

"Then they'll be a little big, but you are supposed to be gaining. You'll wear them with a belt if you have to."

"I didn't get shirts," she pointed out.

"You need underwear too, and we'll have to go to a different store for that."

"Plus dinner," she said sadly. Burying her face in her hands, she sighed.

He let her wallow under the insurmountable weight of it all for only a minute before he reached over and laid his hand on her knee. He squeezed once. It was comforting, right up until he said, "Ready to go back in there for the shirts?"

Gathering the pants, she caught herself midway through

folding them neatly to put back in the thrift shop bag. Wadding them up instead, she tossed them into the backseat.

Marcus rolled his shoulders, shifted in the driver's seat, tsked his tongue against his teeth, but said nothing.

"Yes," she said finally. Taking hold of the door handle, she shouldered the door open again. "Let's do this."

She walked into the store for the third time. At least her stomach wasn't rolling quite as badly as it had been before.

CHAPTER 8

Pony/Anna

They had nachos for dinner. Pony couldn't remember the last time she'd had something so fatty, so simple, and so decadent all at once. She put all the fixings on it, everything she liked—beef, tomatoes, lettuce, sour cream, cheese. Lots and lots of cheese, and even jalapenos. She couldn't remember the last time she'd put jalapenos on anything either, Ethen hated them. Marcus didn't seem to care, and although she'd had two minor melt-downs as she'd helped him cook supper, worrying about whether or not this was what he'd want to eat or if this was how he liked to fix it, when they finally sat down to a heaping plate placed on the table between them, he ate just as much as she did. He wasn't even shy about the jalapenos.

"You like Mexican food?" he asked.

She wouldn't exactly call this Mexican, but she nodded. "I used to eat it all the time. You?"

He smiled, but didn't fall into her trap. "I like Mexican, Chinese, Italian, steak and potatoes. Basically, I like anything that can't move faster than I can. I will say, I'm glad you didn't try to do a low-fat, low calorie salad."

Picking up two chips at once, she stuffed them both in her mouth and although she knew she deserved it, for the first time didn't feel that phantom smack upside the head from Ethen's ghostly hand. "I don't like diet food. It'll serve you right if you get me so used to eating stuff like this that I'm wearing your pants by the end of the month."

He laughed. "Yeah, nice try putting the blame for that on me. I don't care what you weigh, honey, but an unhealthy gain is as bad as being too skinny. Unfortunately for you, the cure is in the basement and I will happily put you down there to run it off."

"I used to jog every morning," she countered, using another chip to scoop up a hefty bite of seasoned beef, cheese and sour cream.

"Your choice or his?"

She shook her head. "He required we stay within a certain weight and punished us with exercise and fasting if we gained, but I mean before I met him. I used to run track in high school and even my first year of college. It was one of my favorite ways to unwind. I'd jog in the morning to get myself in the right headspace for school and then I'd jog at night after studying to relax again. Threaten me with jogging all you want. It's not a punishment."

"Good to know." He smiled and took another bite. "You put on ten pounds, and we'll talk about incorporating jogging into your exercise routine."

She was surprised. "Kind of counterproductive, isn't it? Jogging and trying to gain weight."

"It's not about gaining weight. It's about gaining the right kind of weight, muscle weight, healthy weight. The right ratio of healthy body fat, and above all, it's about finding something you can latch onto mentally and physically that you can control. You're the boss of it. Nobody else, not even me, even if I am making you go down and do it."

"I kind of like the yoga," she admitted.

He glanced at her sideways, then smiled. Reaching over, he stroked her hair. It was wordless praise, but it still lit her up from the inside out.

"I liked it too. Yoga was my first attempt at finding something I could do after I lost my leg," he said. "I didn't get my prosthetic for a while after. I hated the first one so badly, I didn't want to use it. Then I realized I was self-sabotaging and I had to find a way to change my thinking so I could climb out of the slump I'd fallen into."

Folding her arms on the table gave her all the excuse she needed to lean in just a little closer to him as she listened. Over the last week, they'd spent so much time talking about her, that these few unguarded moments when he actually opened up a little to share parts of himself were fast becoming the highlights of her days. "How did you lose your leg?"

"Job went bad," he said honestly. She liked that about him. Marcus could clam up faster than... well, a clam when he wanted to. But for as long as she was willing to be open with him, it seemed he was braced to return the favor. When she asked a question, he answered her with the kind of blunt honesty that made her envy him. He'd given her enough glimpses into his past to know he'd been through hell. A different hell than she, but hell just the same. They had that in common.

"It was a rescue attempt," he explained, pouring a little more salsa over the patch of nachos he was eating. "I had been approached by the family of a guy who was trapped in a religious cult. He wanted to get out, but his wife and baby were being kept away from him and he wouldn't leave them. So I went in, negotiations went bad. They sometimes do. Next thing I knew, everyone had guns and things escalated. Long story short, we did get all three out, but shots were fired and I got hit. The bullet shattered my leg, it got infected, and I ended up..." He gestured through the table at the limb in question, then kept eating. He was quiet for so long, she assumed he was done sharing. She was still trying to figure out what to say when he added, "Long story short, I spiraled. No one wants a dom who can't stand on his own through a scene. Subs want a big cock and a lover with two legs. That sort of thing."

Pony stared at him, uncomprehendingly. That wasn't how she saw him at all. She couldn't imagine anyone seeing anything other than what she saw—a man in full control of himself. A man who had no problem at all taking control of her. His hand on the back of her neck, his sheer size and strength when he loomed over her, commanding all her attention when he wanted it.

He wasn't her dom though, as he was so fond of saying. She didn't dare tell him any of those observations for fear he might read too much into them and withdraw, taking these precious moments that were, to be honest, sometimes the only things keeping her going when her ghostly past rose up to overwhelm her.

"Spencer kept me sane during the worst of it," he said.

She was glad. She was glad he'd had someone there to do that for him, like he was doing for her.

"Tell me," Marcus said, changing the subject. "What's the one thing that you'd like to do when all this is over? What's the one thing that will cement in your mind that you've not only survived all this, but you'll finally be able to live your life the way you want?"

"Anything?"

"Anything at all. No fear of judgments. It's no one's business but yours."

He continued to eat, watching her while she considered it. She didn't need to think very hard, because although she knew she shouldn't want anything like it, she did know what she wanted more than anything else.

"You're not going to like it." She faced the nachos. They were infinitely safer than continuing to let him read her thoughts. He was way too good at it anyway.

"I don't have to like it. It's your life. You're goal."

She scoffed. "I don't have that luxury. The hospital will say..."

"The hospital won't get a say, and neither will the court if I get my say. What is it? What do you want?"

She knew better than to be honest right now. She ought to say something practical—a job, a healthy bank account, her driver's license back and the freedom to go anywhere she wanted. The ability to go into a store and not panic that she wasn't getting the right thing.

"A dom," she softly confessed. "I want to be owned again. I want to serve."

She risked a peek at him, but he was just watching her, chewing.

"I can see that," he said.

His mild acceptance killed her. "You don't think that's wrong?"

"There's a lot of bad doms out there," he said with a sniff. "You landed the king of them, but that doesn't mean your next one won't be one of the good ones. We just have to get you to a point where you can tell the two apart. So, what do you think? Do you want to try tackling a play party?"

She startled so badly, she almost choked on her next chip. "Where?"

"Black Light." His gaze held hers like a challenge. "I know

the manager. Pretty sure I can get us an invite. Might be beneficial for you to get comfortable in that environment again. Relearn the rules. Meet people. Maybe even play, although if we do that, we'll be going in with me as your mentor. You don't play without my permission, and I will vet every single person you talk to and definitely everyone you scene with."

She was too stunned even to continue eating. "Y-you'd let me scene?"

"You're a submissive, Anna. Part of being a healthy person is getting your needs met, and that includes the kink needs. Yes, I'll let you scene. I'll let you meet people in a healthy environment under rules designed to keep you safe. That's part of my job and why everyone pulled together to get me assigned as your guardian."

What would she have to do for that? She couldn't think beyond the impossible carrot being dangled before her.

"When?"

"I think a play party would be a good reward for progress made, don't you?"

Here was the trap, the traitorous part of her brain realized. Here was where he would find a way to yank it out of her reach, because she'd been stupid enough to admit she wanted something.

She tried to shrug, to pretend too late that it didn't matter, but she couldn't. "Reward for what?"

He shook his head. "I'm not sure yet. I think maybe once I see you can safeword or refuse something I tell you to do, then that might be a good indicator that you're ready to try a play party."

Say no to him? He might as well ask her to pluck the sun out of the sky and hand it to him.

"I tried to say no to getting up once," she quipped. "You paddled my butt."

Chuckling, he shook his head. "Yeah, and I'll do it again

too. Detrimental defiance doesn't count. I want you to say no to me for making you eat a jalapeno if you don't like them. Or say no to me if I ask you to sit too close to me on the couch. I want to know you can say no to sitting too close to someone you don't like and that you won't do it just because you want to submit to someone, anyone, because that ghost in your head says you'll be punished if you disobey."

"I bought the pants," she pointed out. "You have no idea how major a no-no that was."

He nodded. "Yeah, I do. You got mad about it. I liked that. Made me proud as hell to watch you march back into the store and get the two things most likely to piss off your ex-dom. You probably got them for that very reason." He took another bite and then wiped his fingers on his napkin. "Yeah, I liked that a lot."

A slow flush of warmth filtered through her, quickening her heart and tightening all the strings now tangling in her stomach. Unlike the strings that liked to make her sick, these were the good kind. She pressed her legs a little tighter together as the warmth flittered down through the slit of her sex, bringing with it a caress of moisture like a gentle fingertip.

Picking up his glass, he took a drink, finishing off the last of his water. "Anna," he commanded as he set his glass down on the table. "Get the bottle of wine from the fridge, please."

The command went down her spine into her legs, which were already tensing to obey. It was a trick, a test, and she knew it. Especially so close onto the heels of this particular conversation.

He'd said please. The argument could be made that she lived here, and really either one of them could have asked the other to get up and get the wine. But up until now, Marcus had never asked her to get anything unless he was rewarding her for something, because he knew how very much she liked to take his orders. How much she ached to be allowed to do it.

She wanted to do it now, ached to obey to the letter of his command. Because she liked him and it was no hardship at all for her to serve him in any way he wanted. In every way, if only he'd want her.

He'd never ask for that, though. She knew just by the way he now watched her, his dark eyes challenging her to take his very obvious bait. Because for all that he would test her, gently pushing for her to break the barbed-wire conditioning Ethen had wrapped her in, he wouldn't deliberately trap her. He was a better man than that. He was the best kind of dom, even if he wasn't hers.

She rubbed her hands on her thighs. "That's mean."

He cocked his head. "How so?"

"You know I want to."

"True."

"How is it wrong to do something when I want to do it?"

"Would it be so wrong to tell me to get up and get it myself?" he countered.

She could have laughed. God, yes. That was wrong on every level. It went against everything she was. Worse, it went against those warming, thigh-tensing, wishful-thinking twitches inside her that whispered tempting thoughts like, if he was willing to ask her to do little things of service—bring him his shoes, fold his laundry, fetch his wine—then someday he might ask her to do other things, like rub his shoulders, help him dress, wash his back in the shower. From there, it was a mouth-wateringly short fall from grace to commands like, kneel down and open your mouth, or bend over the back of the couch, Anna. All spoken in that soft, commanding tone that said he'd make whatever he asked her to do feel more than good.

That tickle of moisture wasn't just a fingertip now, it was

the lash of his tongue, sweeping up through her folds until her clit positively throbbed with wanting.

Her throat tightened, making her sound almost breathless as she said, "Get your own damn wine, Marcus."

Lightning didn't strike her dead on the spot. Who knew?

The corners of his mouth curling, he pushed his chair back, but he didn't get up right away. Instead, his chair creaked as he shifted closer, reaching for her with a slow hand. The caress of his fingers as he combed up the back of her scalp to close his fist in her hair, drawing her head back and forcing her gaze to lock on his sent tingles racing straight to her nipples. Her pussy fluttered, spasms of pleasure so intense as to almost be orgasmic.

He smiled at her gently, his fist in her hair anything but. "Swear at me again, darling. I promise I won't just bust your ass, I'll plug it with increasingly larger butt plugs until I find the one that makes you scream."

Her belly flinched with the intensity of the fluttering that seized her pussy. "Is that our next progress goal?" she heard herself whisper.

His dark eyes heated. His fingers in her hair, tightened holding onto her for a full minute before, almost reluctantly, he let her go.

Standing, he walked into the kitchen and got them both some wine.

Marcus

HE OUGHT to be having a cold shower, not a hot one, but there was no killing his erection tonight. Not after that exchange.

There was no going peacefully to sleep either. He'd lain in bed, the silence in the baby monitor on his bedside table telling him without doubt she wasn't taking advantage of his usual nighttime command: Masturbate if you want to.

She never took advantage of that. If she touched herself even once, not so much as a whisper of sound betrayed her.

He wasn't that dedicated.

From the moment he gave up on sleep and went into his private bathroom, Marcus knew his cock was going to be in his hand and he wasn't stopping, not until he'd expended every last ounce of cum that had his balls drawn up so tight it hurt.

He stood with the hot spray washing down his back, one arm leaning up against the wall to help him keep his balance. His cock was rock hard, standing so high it was almost against his belly. He didn't touch it, letting instead the water sluicing down his chest and running over his tight abdomen, teasing him with the touch he wanted most but knew he couldn't have.

His eyes were open, but that didn't shut out the sight he wanted most, either. Anna would look beautiful on her knees in front of him, worshiping him with her hands and her mouth, her gorgeous blue eyes locked on his face so he would know there was no one else in her mind right now, no one she wanted more in that moment than him and what she was doing for him.

The tickle of the water was a piss poor substitute for her lips, but he could practically feel the way she'd touch him. Lick him. Caress him from balls to shaft, all the way up to the tip where the sensitivity was so heightened that it wouldn't take more than a suckling kiss from her lips to make him shoot into her waiting mouth. Like a high school kid with absolutely no experience and no stamina to withstand the exquisite torture of her lovemaking.

How poetic was that?

Lovemaking.

Making love to her right now wasn't anywhere near the top of his most wanted list. He wanted to fuck her. He wanted to grab her by the hair and pump into her mouth until she was gagging, tears pouring down her cheeks as she struggled to take the full length and girth of him.

He growled, the trickling tickles of water dripping from his face onto his cock so far beyond the sure and certain pump of her hand as she fisted his shaft and worked her beautiful mouth, swirling her tongue around and around his head, as to be completely unsatisfying. He broke down, grabbing his cock in his own hand. He squeezed, needing the pressure to ground him, but the tightness only undid him further. Was that how tight she would be when he finally wrenched her up off her knees and spun her around, shoving her up against these pure white shower tiles? Cheek to the wall, ass out. Making it easy for him to find the heat of her core as he stroked his cock along the seam of her pussy until he found his way in.

He liked hard. He ached to hear that sharp gasp of startled and intense pleasure that his first conquering thrust would wring from her as he shoved himself balls deep inside her.

This shower would sing first with her gasps and then her moaning cries as he took her, pounding until the wet slapping of his hips against her soft ass grew louder. Right now, the only wet slapping he heard was his own furious stroking.

She'd be even tighter, her moans all the more guttural as he took her ass. And he would. He was fond of it, and he had no intention of being gentle when he did it.

Get your own damned wine, Marcus.

She'd never issued a command at him before. Even though they'd mostly been joking around, he considered that great progress on her part... as well as an incredible flirtation. What she'd said had been akin to snapping his dom-y ass with a towel. It had been everything he could do not to come marching back to the table to grab her by the hair and kiss her fucking breathless. He wanted to hear her saying his name, her voice and thighs both quivering with need... God. He stopped, grabbing his cock painfully tight, forcing back the edge of orgasm. It would have been a relief, at this point, but if ever he had her beneath him, he had no interest in granting her a quick release. He wasn't that kind.

Get your own damned wine.

A reluctant smile tugged the corners of his lips again as he recalled every breathless nuance of what she'd said, how she'd spoken, with that trembling quaver in her voice, how she'd looked, raw wanting in her eyes and on her face. She only thought she was raw before. Wait until he was done with her.

Relaxing his grip, he began to stroke again, taking his time now. Slow, long, pumping motions that hit all the places he liked most. He'd find all the places she liked too. Her small, perfect breasts would be the feast he dined on, sucking, licking, spanking, biting, until she was arching and sobbing. He'd mark them. He'd mark her hips and her ass, making sure his fingers left bruises from the force by which he held her, forcing her to keep on riding him long after the pleasure of each subsequent orgasm turned cutting. Pleasure only went so high before it began to court the other side, becoming almost painful in its intensity.

"Shit! Fuck!" He grabbed his cock, but too late. His orgasm hit like a rocket, lancing through every muscle and every nerve as he shot spurt after hot spurt uselessly against the wall. Not in her mouth. Not in her ass. Definitely not in her pussy while she helplessly came along with him, her clenching walls milking every last drop from him.

Shit.

He bent, resting his head against the tiles, the hot water washing down his back.

His good leg was still shaking from the intensity of his release when he finally reached back and shut the water off.

Pushing the shower curtain aside, he sat down on the side of the tub to dry himself off. He was still sitting there long minutes after he was done, staring at the useless stump of his leg and then at the crutches he'd used to come in here, rather than strap his prosthetic back on.

He talked a good game, didn't he? Reaching down, he rubbed the pointed nub below his knee where the ache of the leg he no longer had still liked to remind him of what he'd lost. Yeah, he talked a good game when he was trying to get into her head, but when it came to levels of brokenness, there were worlds of difference between Anna and himself.

Physically, she was perfect, every one of her scars simply the roadmap some lucky man would be able to use as he kissed and caressed his way into her battered heart. Scars didn't matter. They were just the proof sometimes required to remind one that they were stronger than whatever had tried to break them.

Physically, he was still only half a man. Unable even to walk across the room without either his crutches or his prosthetic. A dom in memory only, strong in memory only.

Like Megan, Anna probably wouldn't agree. He wasn't stupid. He knew how she looked at him. He knew the lines between guardian and real-life dom were starting to blur. He'd known they would right from the start, from the instant he first exerted his authority over her. Giving her what she needed in that moment, yes, but dooming them both to the heartbreaking consequences when it came time for him to set her free.

And he would. He knew his job. He knew exactly what the courts would need to deny the hospital's claims that she was so far beyond unfit to take care of herself that releasing her would be akin to killing her. Anna was making great progress. The months she'd spent free of his physical presence while O'Dowell had been in prison had helped in that regard.

So, yes, when the time came, Marcus knew it didn't matter how she looked at him or how hard his cock was, he absolutely was going to let her go. If she wanted to call him, she could, but he'd do right by her. He'd take her to Black Light, he'd even help her find someone there. Someone worthy of her need to submit and serve.

Because after all she'd been through, she needed more and deserved far better than a half-man who'd never again be close to what he used to be.

Except in memory.

CHAPTER 9

Pony/Anna

"You're under my protection," Marcus told her, from the driver's seat. It was night, a little past eight and they'd just come into D.C. It was the first time she'd been back since he'd taken her from the hospital. What was it, only three weeks now? It felt like a lifetime ago.

Her hands folded in her lap, Pony sat straight and tall, rubbing her palms together, trying not to be nervous.

"Did you hear me?" he asked, his tone dropping testily.

He must be nervous too, a realization that only hiked her anxiety. What did he have to be nervous about? He wasn't at all attached to Ethen. People wouldn't look at him the way they were bound to look at her. Would they even recognize her without her harness and pony mask? When she looked in the mirror these days, she barely recognized herself.

"Yes, Sir."

Twelve pounds. That's what she'd gained so far. She was still skinny. Sometimes she could see it in her reflection, but she was almost a hundred pounds now and that was close to what she'd been when last she'd accompanied Ethen to Black Light.

They drove in silence for a time before Marcus leaned forward and turned on her seat warmer. Though she watched the light come on under the button he'd pressed, it didn't hit her what he'd done until the cushion beneath her and at the small of her back began to heat up.

"Why did you do that?" she asked. Early spring in D.C. was practically still winter. It was cold, but the heater had been running since they'd left his house and she wasn't at all chilled.

"To remind you exactly what you'll be feeling if you decide to break any—and I do mean any—of my rules tonight." The look he cast her out of the corner of his eye said he wasn't kidding, despite his choice of words, but instead of scaring her, oddly, she relaxed a little.

"I won't embarrass you," she promised.

"I'm not worried about being embarrassed."

It wasn't her imagination, then. He really was testy.

"What are you nervous about?"

He didn't answer for a long time, not until they reached the right highway exit and he took the offramp onto regular city streets.

"You can talk to anyone you like," he told her. "But if someone makes you uncomfortable and you don't want to talk to them, you tell them they have to get my permission to talk to you. Anyone comes to me with that request, I'll know you'd rather not and I'll make sure it doesn't happen, got it?"

She understood he was setting himself up to be a buffer

between her and anyone likely to blame or harass her for her past association with Ethen O'Dowell. She relaxed even more. "Yes, Sir."

"If you want to stick by me all night, that's fine," he said, and the rules continued on, each one feeling less like a restriction and more like a comfortable blanket wrapping securely around her. "If you want to go off on your own, you can do that too. But you don't play with anyone without my knowledge and permission. You don't arrange your own scenes. You don't negotiate with anyone. You don't say yes or no if someone comes and asks you. You say you are under my protection and all scene negotiations take place with me. Do you understand that?"

"Yes, Sir." She really didn't think she was ready to scene, although there was no mistaking that old familiar zing of excitement just the thought of being asked sent through her. Tiny tingles had lit in the tips of her nipples. She rubbed her hands on her skirted thighs. "Are you going to scene with me?"

He shifted in his seat. "No," he said gruffly. "It wouldn't be appropriate. Not to mention, you deserve a dom who won't fall over if he misjudges his balance in the middle of throwing a flogger."

She looked at him in surprise. "You don't fall over."

"I have," he grimly admitted. "I could. If you scene tonight, you'll do it with someone who can keep up with you."

Blinking twice, she all but turned around in her seat to face him. "You've never had a problem keeping up with me."

If anything, she was the one who always seemed to be running to keep pace with him.

He cast her a stern glance. "I'm not arguing with you about this."

"Good." Facing forward, she folded her arms. "It's a stupid

argument. Quite possibly the stupidest thing I've ever heard you say."

He did more than throw her a glance now. His own surprise giving way to a low, laugh, he adjusted his hands on the wheel. "Say that to me again," he warned. "See how fast I pull this car over."

She didn't doubt he would. Just like she didn't doubt at least one passing motorist would call the cops to report him for paddling her bare ass on the side of the highway. She did, however, roll her hand at him, as if to say 'see, point proven.'

His chuckle grew both softer and darker. "I'm counting that as a word. I also expect you to remember you said it, because just as soon as we're in a place where we won't scandalize the vanillas, we're going to discuss it."

It was still a ridiculous thing for him to say and she regretted nothing. She also let it drop.

Clearing his throat and rolling his shoulders, so too did he. "You can have one drink. One," he continued, laying out the rules, "but you'll come to me to ask for it."

"Yes, Sir." She nodded, but already her lingering irritation at his implied weakness was giving way to the tingling now growing inside her. Her stomach was knotting. The anticipation heightening as they turned from unfamiliar streets onto familiar ones. She was on a route she knew now. They were almost to Black Light, and her nerves were kicking into high gear.

She closed her eyes, trying to imagine the beach and warm sand squishing between her toes. She blew out a slow breath, willing her uncooperative heart to slow. This wasn't going to be any big deal. It wasn't like she was going to walk into the infamous BDSM night club and run straight into Ethen. His ghost, maybe, but not the man and probably not any of his friends. He'd been very careful who he'd let fuck her at the private parties in his house. Yes, a few had been Black Light members, but most had been strangers picked up in parks, malls, or bars. He hadn't wanted anyone at the club to know what sort of things he did, especially to his submissives, in private.

Her hands moved from her lap to her stomach, smoothing imaginary wrinkles from her new dress. It was black, sequined, high in the skirt, low in the back. The whole time she'd been putting on her makeup, she kept looking at herself in this dress and half the time she thought she looked all right. The other half, she thought she looked like a skeleton, with her blonde hair done up in a high ponytail on top of her head and just a few too many ribs showing on her chest where her cleavage should have been drawing eyes.

His hand settled on her thigh, just above her knee, giving her a gentle squeeze. The heat of that sank into her even more effectively than the seat warmer before he said, "You look good, Anna."

She nodded. "You do too."

And he did. He looked better than good in black leather pants, a black, short sleeved t-shirt that fit as if it had been molded to his chest and broad shoulders, and black leather wrist cuffs.

"I'm more used to seeing submissives in cuffs like that," she'd said when he'd first emerged from his room and she saw what he intended to wear to the play party tonight.

"They're convenient," was his mild reply. When she'd only blinked at him, he'd said, "If you misbehave, I don't have to stop what I'm doing and get my bag. I just have to cuff your hands in front of you with these and put you over my knee. Or over a spanking bench, or on a cross. The point is, I've always got restraints and a belt on me, and there isn't a damn thing you can do about it once I decide to use them."

He'd probably be appalled at how deliciously her stomach had dropped when he'd said that, lighting a low pulse of arousal low in her belly and sending a heated flood down to soak the crotch of her panties. Or maybe he did know, because he smiled and winked at her.

"I could use my safeword," she'd belatedly replied.

She'd secretly melted all over herself when he came walking back to her, tipped her chin in his hand so he could look into her eyes as he said, "And that, honey, is why you get to go to the play party tonight."

They turned down the next street, and she saw the parking garage, with the psychic shop just a little further down the street. The well-lit front looked so innocent. How many people not 'in the know' would have absolute fits to discover there was more going on behind that innocuous storefront than palm-readings, mystic stones, incense, and tarot cards?

She rubbed her stomach again, but it was too late to turn around and go back now. They'd come all this way, and to be honest, as nervous as she was, she really didn't want to go back. Would walking in there feel like coming home, or like walking into a tiger's cage?

Finding a place to park, Marcus shut off the car and then sat back, making himself comfortable to wait. It was his habit. The last time he'd got out first to get her door had been the day he'd brought her home. Now, he waited for her to compose herself, to brace herself mentally and physically. Only when she was ready enough to open her own door, did he get out.

"I'm ready," she whispered.

"Good girl."

They got out together, left the parking garage and went down the stairs to street level together, and crossed the street walking side-by-side, because if she fell even once into the trap of walking behind him, there was a paddle on the wall 'with her name on it' and he wasn't shy when it came time to swing it.

"I'm not Ethen," he'd say. "Don't you dare treat me like him."

She tried really hard not to, but if she wasn't consciously thinking about it, the habit was to fall back, let him take the lead, and trail in his shadow. Unseen, unheard, head down. She was comfortable like that. Walking in at his side was the uncomfortable thing. It felt... obvious, scrutinized. Dominant.

Marcus preferred her by his side though, so by his side she did her best to stay. But the closer the building loomed, the harder it was to keep pace with him. Her nervousness was spreading from her hands and her stomach, into her legs. Her knees all but knocked together by the time they reached the front door.

The bell on the shop tinkled as Marcus opened the door for her. It still grated on her every time he did that. In one part, it made her feel special when he did gentlemanly things like opening doors for her, but on the other, she really ought to be the one doing that for—

She squeaked a yelp at the speed at which he grabbed her arm the second they were inside. The world spun as he flipped her under his arm, wrapping her around his hip before the flat of his iron-hard hand came raining down in a sharp storm of slaps that attacked the whole surface of her bottom. The sting escalated into pain with shocking quickness, and it was almost more than she could make herself take in motionless obedience.

She yelped again and grabbed his leg to keep from reaching back. It took more than a few seconds for him to finish, and when he did, it was all she could do not to grab her butt the second he yanked her upright again.

"Are you ever going to roll your hand at me again?" he calmly asked.

"No, Sir." The sting in her bottom was already blossoming into smoldering heat. And yet, her rebel mouth kicked in anyway, "But you'll notice, you didn't fall over."

He tipped his head, studying her for five of the longest seconds of her life. She had a feeling the only thing that saved her from going back over his hip was when the security guard in the back of the shop parted the curtain and looked out at them. "This is a public place, people. Wait until you get downstairs."

Tsking tongue against teeth, Marcus clamped the warm hand he'd just spanked her with on the back of her neck and steered her toward the guard.

"Evening, Luis," he greeted. "How have you been?"

"Doing really good." He brightened, beaming. "Paula is too. She just passed her last exam. In about two hours, someone's going to spell me and she's going to be up on the stage for a reward and a bit of stress relief. She wants to see how many she can take with the bullwhip before she calls it. It'll be intense. When I saw you on the guest list, I thought I'd mention it."

"I'll be there," Marcus told him, shaking his hand and patting him once on the shoulder before taking Anna's arm.

"Why would he mention it?" she whispered, once they were far enough into the tunnel for their voices not to carry back to Luis's station.

"I used to play here," Marcus told her. When she only blinked, still wondering how that fit or why it would matter, he added, "I used to play hard. I've scened with Paula on the stage once or twice. With his consent, of course. Hers too, for that matter."

She couldn't imagine him scening with anyone without their consent. "Does he want you to help with his scene tonight? Was that a hint?"

Sighing, he paused at the door they came to right before

the final security checkpoint and, with his hand on the latch, said, "The last time I scened with them, I did the whipping and he manned the vibrator that got her off. We joked if we ever did it again, we'd swap places."

"Do you want to?" She swallowed past the immediate second-best lump that rose in the back of her throat. Stuffing it way down deep inside her, she knew she had no business feeling this way with him. "Because you can... if you want to..."

"I don't," he told her flatly and opened the door. He motioned her to precede him.

He didn't because he didn't want to, or he didn't because she was there?

She started through the door, but turned back to him halfway through. "I-I don't mind if you—"

"Marcus!" Danny called from the check-in desk. "Long time, no see!"

Marcus raised his hand in a brief wave, though he didn't return the smile. Cutting the wave short, he clapped his hand onto her throat and pulled her right back out into the dimly lit tunnel. The next thing Pony knew, the cool wall was at her back and he had her pinned against.

"I don't want to," he told her sternly, "because I. Don't. Want. To. It has nothing to do with you, and I don't need your permission. You can be nervous, Anna. You can ask me any questions you want, but when I give you the answer, that's it. It's not open for interpretation or argument, and you don't get to ride my ass. Got it?"

"Yes, Sir."

Satisfied, Marcus let go of her throat, opened the door and again they went into the club.

"Marcus," Danny greeted again, still smiling although this time his voice was tinged with amusement. His gaze fell on her, but if there was any recognition for her without her pony gear on, she didn't see it. "How you doing tonight?"

"Fine, you?" Marcus asked, signing them in.

"Can't complain."

The loud thump of the music through the next door was polarizing. Try though she did to wait patiently while the two men settled in for small talk, she found herself drifting closer to take that first long-awaited peek into her old playspace. She wouldn't go inside, she told herself. She'd just look and see who else was here.

With two fingers, she pulled the door open. The night was still early and no one was playing on what few stations she could see from here. But she could see into the bar and that was fairly crowded. The lights were low, the ambient music beckoned. Klara at the bar was hopping, passing out drinks to the submissive wait staff. The shadow of dungeon monitors could barely be detected. Carlson Garvey might be in there; she knew he worked here. Spencer might be up there too, and the thought of seeing him made her mouth run dry. To date, she hadn't had a lot of happy run ins with him, although from everything Marcus said, she knew she had him to thank for her rescue. Without him, it was entirely possible she would now be living on the street somewhere. Or worse, in the home of another dom. Maybe better, possibly worse than Ethen had been.

"Excuse me," a woman said from just behind her, and Pony jumped. She also quickly got out of the way. She should have moved back, but too late she realized her feet had carried her forward, right into the room. The bar area was sprawling out to her left in the distance, and the play area was dead ahead.

"I love play night," the woman giggled at her, as if sharing her exuberance before she took off, dressed in a scarlet and lace negligee and with a play bag slung over her shoulder. She headed out onto the floor, leaving Pony lost amid all the familiar feelings this place had once inspired in her.

Surprisingly, it wasn't the bad feelings she remembered from her last few times coming here, when Ethen had come for the express purpose of humiliating Piggy and then Kitty. It was the feelings from before now building inside her, from that time when this had all been so exciting and new. When Friday nights had been the happy goal that got her through the work week because she knew she was going to start her weekends with a sexy, kinky scene at one of these stations.

She should wait for Marcus.

But her feet drew her deeper into the shadows of the club. Every breath she took was tainted with the smell of leather and oil, liquor, and whatever cleaning solution they used to wipe things down between customers.

She could see all the way into the back of the play area now. Only two scenes were in progress. Two men and a woman were on the stage, her bound wrists hoisted above her head to an attachment in the ceiling. The man behind her was playing with her nipples. She was arching, moaning through her gag, while the man kneeling before her slowly worked his whole hand into her pussy.

A naked man in a sensory hood with his arms bound behind his back was bent over a spanking bench. His dominant lover was standing right behind his already bright red ass, pants undone and lubing up his cock. The Dom gave his submissive's ass a no-nonsense slap and without any further preparation or gentleness, in he went. It might have been a punishment. The submissive's strangled shout certainly indicated it hurt, but his dom only grabbed his hips and rode him furiously. And even from where he was, Pony could see the red ball the submissive held clutched in his bound hands—the safeword for someone gagged. He writhed and wailed, but didn't let it fall.

She'd missed this. All the sights, smells and sounds. Submissives being alternately tormented and taken care of by those who topped them.

The sound of shattering glass startled her, and Pony snapped her attention back to the bar to find herself standing not ten feet away from Puppy, of all people.

Vague memories of being forced to come here with Carlson Garvey just before… the unthinkable had happened… before losing Ethan. He'd helped Puppy get a job bussing tables at Black Light. She never dreamed Puppy would be able to hold down a job.

That was Pony's first ungracious thought. Her second was even darker: would Puppy even want her here? Because of all the menagerie girls, it was Puppy she had wronged the most. What had she done these last eight months while Ethen was in prison, except ride Puppy, bully her, forcing her again and again to visit their abuser because she herself couldn't bear to go alone? Or to be seen by him as disobedient. She'd slapped Puppy, right across her face and for no better reason than because she'd been so wrapped up in her own unhappiness, her own unrequited love for a man incapable of ever returning such an emotion. There was no way Puppy would want anything at all to do with her anymore, and she had earned that.

Pony almost took a step back, ready to put that separation in between them so it wouldn't hurt quite as much when the inevitable rejection came, but then Puppy's face changed from wide-eyed, open-mouthed shock into one of ecstatic glee. She screamed a happy squeal, throwing out her arms and practically flinging her tray as she leapt through the crowd to throw her arms around Pony's shoulders.

"You're not mad at me?" she whispered, the wonder of it stealing some of the weight from her shoulders as Puppy's arms tightened. That the other girl was crying, she didn't realize until Puppy pulled back. Her face was wet and her eyes glistening as she laughed.

"No." She let go of Pony long enough to swipe away the tears with both hands. She laughed again. "No, I'm not mad. I've thought about you every day."

Throwing her arms around Pony again, she hugged her even tighter and this time, Pony hugged her back. Something inside her broke, and her tentative embrace became fierce. She didn't cry, but she could feel the urge right there in the back of her throat, rising perilously higher the harder Puppy hugged her back.

Someone cleared his throat.

They let go of one another and Puppy turned, a blush already rising up into her face as she looked first at Spencer, standing at the bar with his arms folded across his chest and his customary frown not softening an ounce.

"How many glasses did we just break?" he asked.

Her blush deepened. "Um... right. I'm sorry."

Ducking her head, she reclaimed the tray she'd thrown from an equally stern dom sitting at one of the couches next to a submissive who was now rubbing her arm.

"Sorry," she told them both, then dropped to pick up the pieces of shattered glass from the floor. "I'm very sorry."

"It was my fault," Pony broke in. "I—"

"Walked in the door," Spencer finished for her. "Yes. I saw."

A warm hand settled on her shoulder, startling her until she saw Marcus.

"Reacquainting yourself with old friends, I see," he said mildly. And she was so glad he was there. The sternness of Spencer's gaze didn't soften for him either, but it wasn't locked solely on her anymore either.

"She's taking the blame for shit she didn't do," he said. "Seems to be par for the course with the Menagerie. Don't—" he cut Puppy off before she could say she was sorry again.

"Just get a broom and don't cut yourself. I'm out of band aids. Why am I always out of fucking band aids when you're here?"

He turned, stalking past the bar and down the short hall to his office.

"He doesn't like me." Pony didn't mean to actually say that, but once it was out she couldn't exactly say she'd lied.

"Sure, he does," Marcus disagreed. "That was absolutely his 'I like you' face. When he doesn't like someone, his eyes turn jet black and his horns, tail and pitchfork all come out."

The unexpectedness of his joke almost made Pony laugh, right up until Spencer's terse voice snapped out from his office, "Those broken glasses are coming out of your paycheck, Cynthia!"

Pony looked to her friend, who after a startled pause, let out another squeal and scampered back to the bar with her tray full of broken glass. "Klara, Klara! Did you hear that? I get a paycheck now!"

"I heard!" Taking the tray, the female bartender passed a broom and dustpan over the bar to her. "Sweep the floor, sweetie."

"You can catch up with your friend later," Marcus told her. "Come on."

Careful to fall into step beside rather than behind him, Pony followed him on a slow tour of the room.

"How do you feel?" he asked, keeping his voice soft as he surveyed each of the two scenes still playing out, completely undisturbed by the minor commotion she had caused at the bar.

"Nervous," she confessed. "Glad to be back. Scared at the same time."

He paused to watch the woman on the stage as she arched, keening wildly through clenched teeth as the dom on his knees before her worked her clit with his thumb and his fisting hand with slow, steady pumps, gradually forcing her to take more and more until she writhed in the throes of hip-bucking orgasm.

"Would you let me do that to you?" he asked, not looking at her.

"Yes," she said without hesitation.

"Do you *want* me to do that to you?" he rephrased.

Not especially. She'd been fisted once. Once had been plenty. And yet, she couldn't imagine Marcus doing anything in this place that would... what, hurt? She could positively picture him doing all kinds of things to her that would hurt, at least a little. She could see him putting her over the spanking bench. Easily, in fact. He'd spanked her already and his spankings hurt plenty. Usually, he was correcting her when he did it though, and corrections were meant to hurt. She could see him tying her up, putting a hood on her like the submissive man now grunting under the vigorous thrusts of his Dom. The pain of that rough entry must have eased by now, because his cries were more like groans of lust and when she glanced his way, she could see his cock straining at the confines of the cock cage he wore.

She could see Marcus doing that to her too, and the low swirl of heat that blossomed into instant throbs between her legs was all the proof she needed to know she'd have bent herself into submission for that too. Her pussy, her ass... it didn't matter, she'd have let him do it all.

Her gaze returned to the woman, her body jerking in the lingering spasms of her orgasm. That was how she would end, she realized, if she let Marcus top her. Because even if it did hurt, there was no doubt in her head that he would ensure it ended in an orgasm so powerful that all she could do was wilt in his arms and twitch.

"I would let you do it," she said honestly. "Once. So I can see if it's different from the last time."

He nodded. "Let me change my question." He pointed to

the two men in specific. "Would you let me ask any two men in this room to string you up on that stage when those three are done, and put you through the same..."

"Please don't," she said immediately, her hand moving to her flipflopping stomach. She pressed, trying to still the tense acrobatics.

"Would you want to do it?"

"No." She didn't need to think about that at all.

"Would you do it if I told you to?"

She could lie and say no, but they both knew she would. When it came to being told what to do, it was almost impossible for her to say no. "Probably," she said unhappily.

"Until that changes, I'm going to be your protector every time we come here. But we're going to work on that together, and eventually, we will get past it. Come on, let's walk around."

He took her slowly through the room, past all the equipment currently not being used while she pointed out which stations she'd tried and what she'd done. She didn't go into many details. For all that she'd been coming here for years, even those memories which a few short weeks ago she would have described as happy ones really weren't. She'd thought she'd been so fortunate just to have Ethen consider her worthy of scening with in public, and especially when he did it himself. But looking back, almost all of them had at least one aspect that turned her stomach, tightened her throat, made her uncomfortable.

"Ready for that drink?" he asked.

"God, yes." She was ready to stop thinking about ghosts. She turned her back on the room as if turning her back on the awkward memories were just as easy. It wasn't. They followed her to the bar, where Marcus found a two-person couch up against the wall for them to talk.

"Are you going to be here a while?" Puppy asked when she came to get their drink order. "Can we talk later?"

Pony looked to Marcus. "I… I don't know how long we'll be here, but I'd like that."

"We'll be here until it becomes too much," Marcus told her.

Puppy grinned. "What can I bring for you?"

"Nothing, thank you," he told her. "Anna will be serving me tonight." He looked at her. "Would you like that?"

That pulse of warmth that the ghosts had done their best to kill returned instantly and with a vengeance, lighting up every one of her nerve endings as she sat beside him.

"Yes, Sir," she whispered.

"Just drinks," he asked, "or would you like to try a scene?"

With him? Her heart stumbled, the pulsing throb taking hold of her clit and owning it. "Doing what?"

"Serving me," he said bluntly.

She turned to look out across the play stations. The couple on the stage were done, and a worker was cleaning their area. The two men on the spanking bench were done too. The sub was now wrapped in a blanket and his Dom's steadying arm as he unsteadily walked, dazed and flying high in subspace, toward the aftercare cubicles. Another couple were setting up their own scene at a St. Andrews' cross, the top digging his floggers out of his bag while the submissive stripped out of her already scant clothing.

"Do you trust me?" Marcus asked, and she quickly returned her gaze to his.

Was this another test? Did he expect her to say no, because it would be a lie if she did.

She opened her mouth to say yes, but then stopped. The problem here wasn't did she want to spend the evening on her knees before him, fetching him drinks, fetching whatever he wanted, doing whatever he wanted. The problem was when the scene was over, how was she supposed to stop doing what she loved so much and go back to 'I am not your dom'?

She needed to tell him no, for her own sake and survival. And yet, what finally came pouring out of her was very different. "I'd like that very much."

She wasn't just playing with fire. She was dousing herself in gasoline first.

CHAPTER 10

Marcus

He wasn't playing with fire, he was playing with a bomb. And yet, his hands felt perfectly steady as he reached for each item of clothing that Anna handed him. He'd have preferred to keep her dressed, especially in the middle of Black Light where already she was attracting attention from single tops looking for something—someone—to do tonight. That she would eventually find someone to play with had been one of his biggest reasons for coming here. Ethen was a shark, and she'd gotten bit. Part of her healing would have to involve getting back in the water, or she'd wind up afraid of the ocean forever.

He'd been braced for this, or so he'd told himself. He'd known she would attract eyes from the moment she stepped onto the floor. She was still too thin, but the weight she'd thus far gained had done wonders to help fill out some of her skeletal gauntness. The dark rings under her eyes were little more than shadows. The hollow boniness of her cheeks wasn't quite as pronounced. And she was pretty. She was more than pretty. She was taller than most women, and her thinness just helped to dress her in the envy and illusion that she could perhaps be or once have been a runway model.

Perhaps he should have braced himself a little harder, because the reality of actually having her here was different from what he'd imagined. He didn't like the way people were looking at her. Some were even whispering, not that those people mattered. He was pretty sure Ethen's name was on half their lips, but people would be people and he honestly couldn't have cared less about the gossip. It was his fellow doms that he was starting to have a problem with, and he had no idea what about that rankled him. Of course, they wanted to watch this. Anna was gorgeous, submissive, and she was taking off her clothes with the quiet acceptance of a woman who'd spent so much time naked in front of people that she no longer even thought about it. As he'd told her to, she left her heels on and now stood before him in nothing but her thigh-high stockings and shoes.

Small wonder they were staring.

Marcus could barely take his eyes off her either. His fingers itched to do what his eyes were, explore her, the curve of her small, perfect breasts, the slender plane of her belly, that v of bare flesh where not a trace of pubic hair had been left to stand guard over her naked pussy.

Oh now, there was a shadow he wouldn't mind getting lost in for a while. It took everything he had to let his gaze continue moving over her, the way an interested dom would and should gaze upon anyone willing to gift him with the pleasure of their body. No stopping, no lingering. No thinking about how she would feel beneath his wandering fingertips, or how she would taste.

Or how she would sound, moaning his name as he slid his

tongue, his fingers, his cock up inside the tight, slick well of her body.

Hot against his thigh, his cock was already swelling in anticipation.

This was a dangerous game, and he knew it, just like he knew he should have someone else do this for him. For him to play the Dom in this scenario was an unnecessary complication doomed to bite them both in the ass. He could tell himself he was doing this to make absolutely sure nothing went wrong during her first gentle reintroduction back into the lifestyle, but he knew better. He could monitor this scene just as competently from the sidelines. So why insinuate himself into it?

Because just thinking about cruising this room in search of another dom had grated straight up his spine until he could physically feel the skin-flaying between his tensing shoulders.

It was because this was so important, he told himself. He couldn't afford for her to have a serious backstep, especially since of all his methods *this* was the one—should it come out in court—most likely to get him into hot water.

He waited, watching her, saying nothing while she took a deep breath, composing herself the way he'd told her to before, with all the grace that only years of practice could give a woman, lowering herself from high heels onto her knees. Her head bowed, her hands turned palm-up on her thighs, her legs slightly spread.

He liked the shadow. He liked the illusion of being the first to travel that hidden highway in search of all her private treasures.

Who knew, she might actually be nervous about this. Their negotiation had been the shortest of his entire experience. If he hadn't been living with her, he never would have stopped it so prematurely. In its entirety, it had consisted of:

"Is there any place you would like me to refrain from touching?"

The way her chest quickened as she took her shallow breaths, the flutter of her racing heart in the hollow of her throat, and the blush, so faint it could barely be seen under the dim ambiance lighting of Black Light's bar—they all told as much of the truth as her words when she finally said, "No, Sir."

"Think carefully," he'd told her. "Be honest, because I intend to make that one question the focus of my scene. I'm going to touch you. Every inch of you. If the thought of me shoving my fingers or my cock in your mouth, your pussy, or your ass bother you, now's the time to say so. Again, is there any place you'd rather I not touch?"

That flutter of her heart was racing harder, her breathing just that much shallower than before. Her voice had a slight tremor when she said, "No, Sir."

"What are your hard limits?"

He saw it in her eyes as she tried and failed to find something to deny him. He had all kinds of hard limits and knew exactly what he'd never do to her, even when she shook her head.

"Get naked," he'd told her. "Everything but your shoes and stockings. When you're ready to begin, you can let me know by kneeling. That's when our scene will start."

Now, here she was, on her knees and waiting, her visibly pounding pulse adding to his excitement. Her hands were resting on her thighs, palms turned up in open submission, eager to be commanded. He could just have devoured her.

"Bourbon," he ordered. "Straight, please. They know what I like. You may bring something for yourself, if you like."

Even as he said it, he knew she wouldn't. Her nipples were tight little beads and the tips of her fingers were trembling ever so faintly. She was finally being allowed to do the one thing she ached most to do, and which had been denied to her for almost a year. She wasn't about to waste a second of this on herself, which meant he'd have to be extra watchful to ensure her care.

As if watching her was any kind of hardship. She rose to stand with such smooth grace, her lithe body pure poetry of motion as she walked away from him to the bar. Naked and scantily dressed women were not an uncommon sight in Black Light. It made picking out the experienced doms from the novices and wannabes through the bar easy. Experienced doms in conversation with their own submissives barely glanced her way. Those that did, admired briefly and then went back to what they were doing. To the inexperienced, Anna was irresistible. Eye candy that drew longing looks from all directions.

That was the point of this, a little voice in the back of his head whispered. It was hard to hear it over the surge of possessiveness that immediately rocketed through him.

He didn't like any of the men he saw following her with their hungry eyes.

He didn't know any of them either. Finding her a qualified dom had to be part of the ultimate goal that marked her healing progress, and yet there wasn't a soul in the bar that he didn't instantly judge on the opposite end of that spectrum the second he clapped eyes on them. Upwards and including the blond man in black leathers who did a double-take when Pony stepped up to the crowded bar beside him and patiently waited for Klara to notice her.

The way he looked her up and down sent the electrified need for movement jolting down his spine and into his legs. Marcus almost came up off the couch, but the man hadn't done anything wrong. He hadn't done anything period, and yet that need to storm across the room and insert himself between them was almost more than he could swallow.

He wasn't even the jealous type. Or at least, he never had been before.

Rolling his shoulders, Marcus cracked his knuckles and forced himself to calm back down. This was ridiculous. Having people look at her, admire her—want her—that was exactly what she needed. It was what he'd come here tonight with every intention of giving her. It was a shot of much needed confidence. A return to normal for her, the validation all submissives craved and proof that they were beautiful in the eyes of someone. Wanted, by someone.

She needs this. Sit here and take it.

Jesus, the man just touched her wrist, a slight tap of the finger to get her attention but which anyone who knew anything about consent in places like this ought to know was forbidden as hell. Look all you want, you don't touch without permission. Ever.

He almost came up off the couch again, but too late. Anna glanced at him. In her heels, she was slightly taller than he was, but only just. The guy was smiling, introducing himself. Anna's face was a mask, but he could tell by the way her fingers tightened where she was holding onto the edge of the bar and the soft flush that stole up into her cheeks, that he'd just paid her a compliment.

Where was the pride that he was supposed to be feeling for her, right now? Marcus forced himself to relax, forced his fists to unclench and was almost too late in donning his own neutral mask before she glanced uncertainly in his direction.

I'm right here, he let his stare assure her. *Go ahead. Talk to him. You're doing good, honey.*

She was doing everything right, everything he'd hoped would happen her first time back into the scene. What the hell was wrong with him? There was little in this interaction that should be making him this upset. Yes, that unwanted touch was out of line, but depending on how long the man had been in the scene, it might have been nothing more than a minor mistake. One easily corrected by just informing him of the rules he should have read and signed acknowledgement of when he first became a member.

"You look ready to kill."

Startled, Marcus glanced right just as Spencer dropped to sit on the couch beside him. Crossing his ankle over his knee, Black Light's manager made himself comfortable, a tumbler of whiskey in his hand which he rested lightly on his thigh.

"I'm fine," Marcus dismissed, his attention returning to the bar.

"She looks different," Spencer said after a moment.

It shouldn't have rankled that his old friend had noticed, but it did. What the hell was wrong with him? She was naked, she was gorgeous, she was a single submissive in a den full of solitary doms—if people weren't looking, she'd have been justifiably crushed.

Struggling to quash this unfamiliar jealousy, Marcus rolled his shoulders again. "She's making good progress."

"Then why do you look pissed?"

"I'm not pissed. I'm proud."

"That's your proud look?"

"This is my waiting for a god-damn drink look. Son of a b —" Too late Marcus clamped his mouth shut, but the damage was already done and Spencer was also now taking note of another dom, making his move across the crowded bar toward Anna. Watching his approach was like having sharpened razors scraping up his spine. Every single cut was painfully slow and sinking in deep. "She's just getting a god damn drink," he growled under his breath.

"She's naked, in a dungeon, and without a collar."

Siddling up to the bar on her other side, the older man now introduced himself, ignoring the look the first dom shot him as he smiled at Anna.

Her grip on the bar got a little tighter, but otherwise Anna didn't move. When he said something to her, she replied.

Look at me, Marcus willed her. Give me a sign of distress.

She was aggravatingly uncooperative in that regard.

At last Klara worked her way down the bar to where she'd been waiting. Both doms jumped to get her a drink, but Klara's nod was for Anna and the drink when she returned a short few minutes later was obviously his.

"Good girl," Spencer said under his breath, startling Marcus just before he embarrassed himself further by echoing the same.

The younger man tried to touch her arm again, an attempt to reclaim her attention from the other man who was speaking to her. It was the older dom who immediately squashed that attempt, blocking that touch with a point of his hand. Chastened, the younger man retreated.

His drink cupped in her hands, Anna paused long enough for the older dom to finish what he was saying. Whatever she said in return was brief and then she left him there, watching hungrily after her as she walked directly back to him. As she knelt on the floor directly in front of his feet, the older dom looked directly at Marcus for the first time.

"Please stop stabbing him with your eyes," Spencer chuckled under his breath.

"I'm not." Taking his drink from her offering hand, Marcus held the other man's assessing stare without blinking. "I'm simply letting him know I won't take his bullshit."

The club manager laughed again, no longer bothering to keep it under his breath this time. "What makes you think—"

"Because he's a guy," Marcus cut him off, not at all comfortable with how irritated this whole process was making him. "Men are naturally full of bullshit, especially where women are involved."

And Anna was beautiful. The bullshit around her was bound to be deeper than most.

This was ridiculous. He'd been a protector before. He'd supervised at least half a dozen scene negotiations between newbie submissives and their potential play partners. Why was this different? It annoyed him that he couldn't put his finger on a solid reason.

It really annoyed him that this all was amusing Spencer as much as it seemed to be and now—shit—shoving off the bar, the other dom was heading his way.

Fuck.

Tossing the drink back, Marcus drained his glass and hoped like hell it would settle his nerves.

"Excuse me." There was challenge in the other dom's eyes when he paused in front of Marcus, his foot bare inches from Anna's hip. He stuck his hand out in greet. "Name's Anders. Pony says you're her protector and any requests for a scene need to go through you."

Fuck, piss, bugger… Marcus fought not to glare until the man retracted his unaccepted handshake. Frozen at his feet, there were goosebumps on Anna's skin. She was excited. He did his best not to grit his teeth and gestured to a nearby empty chair instead. "What kind of scene?"

"What kind of scenes does she enjoy?" was the other man's affable response. Pulling a chair up to the couch, he made himself comfortable. "I'm pretty open. I enjoy impact, mild breast and pussy torture—"

Those prickles of irritation had turned into razor blades, cutting sharply into him. "Not a chance," he cut in.

Anders held up non-threatening hands. "I also enjoy violet wands, orgasm control—"

"Not a chance there, either." The blades cut mercilessly deeper.

"Sensory play," Anders continued. He paused to study

him. "I confess, protocol and service subs have been an infatuation of mine for years. I'd just like to get to know her better."

Marcus didn't take his gaze off the other man, but Anna was still kneeling beside him, her head still bowed, her nipples still peaked with interest. She hadn't moved, but he knew she was interested. More than that, he knew she was excited. Someone wanted to play with her, and she hadn't had this in such a long time.

He should be letting her do it, but instead, he couldn't seem to stop himself from sniping at the man. "You can't come up with a more definitive scene than that?"

He hadn't meant to do that. His tone dripped with disapproval, and he had no reason for it. But try telling that to the pulsing heat of possessiveness building inside his chest, crushing his lungs, until every breath he took felt weighted with jealousy. He wasn't even a jealous man, or at least he never had been before.

The other dom arched a surprised brow. He blinked, sitting back in his chair as he studied Marcus. His eyes narrowed slightly, but his hands remained loosely folded and relaxed in his lap. "Perhaps I misunderstood the situation? Is she not available to scene?"

"She is, and she can scene with whomever she wants," he corrected, wishing he could silence the knives digging in deep between his shoulder blades, but it was only getting worse. Stronger, and more irrational. He knew better than this, and yet he couldn't stop himself. "But I'm her protector. It's my job to make sure the person she scenes with knows what he's doing, so she doesn't get hurt. I don't know you."

"Fair enough, let me tell you more about me." His expression made that concession both look and sound like a challenge. "I've been a dom for about seven years. I've had—"

"When was your first scene?" Marcus cut in.

"I just told you, I started getting into this about seven years ago."

"No, you said you'd been a dom that long. This might come as a shock but there's a difference between knowing how you identify and actually having the experience to back it up. You don't magically become a dom just because you read Fifty Shades or got hard on during the movie. You've got the terminology down, I'll give you that. But while that might impress the other newbies, I'm a whole different animal."

"I'm not a newbie," Anders said stiffly.

"I value my submissive too much to take that chance. Fuck off," Marcus told him bluntly. He deliberately did not look at Anna. He didn't want the guilt cutting into him now too as tiny hints of unhidden disappointment tipped her head or dipped her shoulders.

"Fair enough," Anders said again, but his darkening face was anything but accepting. He glanced at her once, which sent a whole new wave of possessiveness prickling up Marcus's spine, and then he got up and stalked away. Much to the delight of the dom he himself had slighted, watching all this from a distance at the bar.

"Well," Spencer said, hiding his smile behind his almost empty glass. "At least you let him sit down."

"Fuck off," Marcus told him too, albeit without the same degree of rancor that Anders's proximity had inspired.

Chuckling, the club manager heaved himself up off the couch. He followed after Anders, patting the man once on the back as he passed on his way back to Klara at the bar. No doubt to spread the 'delightful' news of Marcus's unseemly behavior.

Gritting his teeth, Marcus shifted, but there was no comfort to be found on this chair or relief from the razors scraping him raw inside. "Did you like that guy?" he asked, forcibly keeping his tone and his expression as neutral as he could manage. "Do you want to try doing something with him?"

She didn't look up, but her hands on her knees tightened. He saw the twitch in her fingers before she made herself relax again. "I... not if you don't like him."

He wasn't entirely sure there was anyone he would like in this place. He cast irritably around him, looking from man to man. Trying to spot someone—anyone—who didn't make the knots in his gut tighten or the razors sharpening themselves on his nerves worse. Jamie was setting up the spanking bench. Marcus might let him play with her, but then Jamie was a submissive and completely out of the question.

What the fuck was wrong with him?

"Go get him," Marcus told her gruffly. "Tell him to come back, then go to the bar and get me another drink." He was going to need it.

Raising her head for the first time, Anna looked at him with those brilliant blue and somewhat bewildered eyes of hers. "If you don't want me to play—"

"In about two seconds your first scene here is going to be a bare-ass spanking," he snapped, even more gruffly, "and I promise you won't like a bit of it. What did I just tell you to do?"

That she didn't immediately just to obey was both a source of unparalleled irritation and pride. She had made real strides since coming to live with him.

Setting his drink aside, he very deliberately stood up, squaring off against her. "One," he growled.

She blinked, openly startled. "Are... are you counting to three?"

"Two." He started to take off the leather cuffs he was wearing.

No doubt remembering how he'd already said he'd use them on her if she misbehaved tonight, she got up. Any other submissive would have scrambled to obey, but not Anna. She rose in a single, fluid motion and walked away from him with a stride that was both hurried and yet as seemingly unhurried as a woman on the verge of her Dom's punishment could be. Exactly as Ethen had trained her to do.

That annoyed him even more. What the hell was wrong with him?

Throwing himself back down on the couch, he snatched up his empty glass and tossed it back, draining what few drops were left in the bottom because it was better than rubbing his face like the hopeless loser he was behaving to be. He set the empty tumbler aside again before he was tempted to let his spiking temper get the best of him and throw it.

That little bit of weight she'd put on was doing wonders on her ass and hips. She was fleshing out. She looked good walking away from him, something he supposed he ought to start getting used to.

His jaw clenched.

It clenched again as he watched her approach Anders where he'd sidled up to the bar to lick his wounds. She touched his shoulder as she neared and he glanced at her first, then him, and then back to her again.

Get a fucking handle on it, he told himself firmly as the other dom, after only a slight hesitation, turned to come back to him. As she'd been told, Anna stayed at the bar to order another drink.

Closing his eyes, he blew out a pent-in breath and tried to find his center of calm.

Walking on a white sandy beach. Waves lapping at the shore. Hot sun beating down on his shoulders and the salty sea air playing with his hair...

"Changed your mind?" Anders asked.

"She isn't a masochist," Marcus said, calm not quite attained but opening his eyes anyway. He glared at the other dom, knowing everything he was feeling right now wasn't this man's fault and yet unable to swallow it back. "She doesn't like pain, so it's only used for punishment."

Anders blinked. "All right."

"You don't punish her," Marcus continued. "That's my job, not yours."

Nodding, he said, "Agreed."

"She craves being touched." He would hate himself forever for sharing that with this man. It added an extra gruffness to his tone when he followed that by saying, "This is her first time back after a very long and miserable situation. If she wants to tell you about it sometime in the future, that's on her, but you aren't to ask about it. You can touch her tits and her ass, but you keep your hands off her pussy. No insertables. No orgasm control."

"Got it."

"One more thing," Marcus said, hating himself even more. "Screw this up and not only will you never scene with her again, but I'll fucking break you in half. You got that, too?"

It was hard to tell if the other man was more offended or surprised, but in a blink he shuttered that emotional behind a thin veneer of irritation and an even thinner smile of acceptance. "You're the boss."

Yes, he was. He was also being unreasonable. Had the shoe been reversed, he'd have told himself to fuck off and walked away. But Anders didn't do that. He went back to the bar, took the drink Klara had just handed Anna out of her hand, handed it to a passing server with a generalized point in his direction, and then he took her arm and led Anna out onto the play-space floor.

She quickly looked his way, and Marcus nodded so there would be no doubt in her mind that it was all right for her to go with him. He even tried to smile, but that was asking too much. When his drink came, he stood up and made his way around the periphery of the room, following at a distance while Anders took her into the very back area. He chose a massage table before pausing long enough to exchange words with her.

He'd have thought Anna nervous the way she glanced around the dungeon before her gaze found him. He let her see him as he took up a position along the wall, near enough to see everything, even in the dimly lit atmosphere of the dungeon, just far enough not to intrude on what that other man was about to do to her.

His leg ached.

Finding an empty chair, he sat down.

His hands were aching too. It was all he could do to watch as Anders gave Anna directions, and then walked away from her. He wanted to find all kinds of fault with that, but he knew what the other dom was after. And within moments, he'd returned. Sure enough, with his play bag slung over his shoulder.

He wished he could hear what Anders was saying to her.

Marcus scoffed at himself and his own wayward reactions. Hell, right now, he wished he were Anders.

CHAPTER 11

Pony/Anna

"*Have* you any history of reactions to lotions?"
Anders asked.

Pony shook her head and watched in growing anxiousness as he popped the top on the bottle, the fragrance of vanilla wafted through the air even before he held it to her nose.

"Yes?" he asked. "No?"

She nodded. He was doing everything right, and yet this didn't feel right. She felt uneasy when she should have been relaxed, aroused even by the prospect of her first scene in so long. Especially with a man other than Ethen. Goosebumps were racing across her skin, but not because she was excited or aroused. She didn't know what she was feeling, apart from almost wanting this to just be over.

Anders smiled and she tried to smile back. "Lie down on your stomach," he told her.

He gave her bottom a playful smack as she dutifully rolled

over on the table, positioning herself face down with her head pillowed on folded arms.

Anders made no move to warm the oil in his hands before drizzling a cold line straight down her back. She sucked a short breath, her body tensing. The cold should have titillated her. She needed to try harder to want this and not be so aware of her surroundings. It was so weird, though. At the bar while basking in the unexpected attention of two doms vying one another to scene with her, the prospect of playing had been exciting. But now, something just felt… off.

Closing her eyes, she tried to concentrate on the tickling drops of oil rolling off her. Still, it didn't feel erotic or even particularly pleasant when he leaned over her, the heat of his hands settling on her shoulders as he asked, "Have you been a good girl, Pony?"

For just a second, her name on his lips zapped her straight out of Black Light and back into Ethen's living room. She felt just like she had while facing down a long evening of entertaining someone her Master had picked for her.

She told herself she was shrugging that feeling off her, not Anders hands. "I've tried to be."

A wave of goosebumps prickled up her arms and across the back of her neck when he caressed her spine, coating his hand and her skin both in slick oil. Painfully aware that several voyeurs were drifting into the back to watch, she tried to school her mind into the right frame. This was supposed to be fun, not a chore she had no choice but just to get through.

What was wrong with her? Her skin was crawling, the unwantedness of his touch caressing from her waist up to her neck. She had to fight not to shrug away again as he swept her long hair over her shoulder, tucking it into the fold of her arms so as to protect it from the oil while he massaged her shoulders, arms, neck, even her hands. Again, he was doing everything right, taking the time to lift each hand and thoroughly rub the oil between her fingers, but it wasn't his touch she wanted to feel.

The realization startled her. Once upon a time, she would have been giddy, bouncing off these dark painted walls for a chance to scene—with anyone, doing anything—so excited just to be living in the scene. And yet here she lay, frozen under a touch she didn't want and couldn't make herself get lost in. Where was Marcus? Was he watching this?

"No," Anders censored, planting an oily hand on her head and forcing her back down. "Lie still."

She obeyed, flinching at the chill as he drizzled another line of oil down the backs of each of her legs.

He was using a lot of oil. Like a good dom, he was trying to use every sensation to heighten her experience. Could he sense she wasn't into this? Not wanting to be the reason this scene failed, she squeezed her eyes shut and tried again to lose herself in enjoyment that just wouldn't come. She had to roll her lips to keep back an uncomfortable grunt as he deepened the massage, actually hurting as he rubbed the soles of her feet.

"I should be doing this to you," she said softly. Maybe that was her problem. Maybe this would be more fun were she the one taking care of him.

He smacked her bottom again, this time hard enough to make her breath catch. "Hurts more when you're oiled up, doesn't it?"

"Yes, Sir."

"Then let me do what makes me happy. I'm tempted to tell you to take it like a good girl, but we'll save that for another time." He leaned over her, the brush of his breath making her skin prickle when he added, "After all, that's something to be said when you're bouncing on a hard cock, isn't it?"

Her gut tightened as again she was snapped out of Black Light. This time, it was more than just a ghost of a feeling. For just a second, the dungeon furniture around them became Ethen's living room furniture and the shadow form of a man seating himself on a spanking bench to watch became the Master of the Menagerie himself. Judging her and her ability to please.

Don't make me ashamed of you. That was what he'd say.

She felt sick.

Red.

The club safeword leapt to her lips, but refused to go any further. She locked her jaw before she embarrassed herself or Eth—Marcus. *Marcus!*

This was ridiculous. She squeezed her eyes shut again, struggling not to squirm as Anders worked his now deeply uncomfortable touch up the backs of her legs to her ass. She grabbed the padded edge of the table when he slid both hands up over her ass, cupping her there, squeezing and very deliberately spreading her ass cheeks apart. He held her like that for just a second too long for it to be an accident or a massage.

Her breathing quickened. She tightened, snapping her head over on her arms to stare into the crowd. She schooled her features, hiding her fast-rising panic the way only a good menagerie girl could.

"Are you sure you don't like spanking?" Anders asked, adjusting his grip on her ass as he rubbed. "You've got the perfect butt for it."

He squeezed again, prizing her open again, sending the panic spiraling wildly as his thumb skimmed the rim of her anus.

"Beautiful pussy too."

He slid his hand between her legs and suddenly, Anna broke free. She scrambled to sit up, but every instinct screaming inside her—stop, wait, red—was broken. It wouldn't come up to her mouth.

Anders looked at her in surprise. "What's the matter?"

She'd never felt more stupid in her life. She was ruining his scene. He'd been doing everything right and she was ruining it.

"Did I do something wrong?" he asked. "Do you want to stop?"

She needed to apologize, but she couldn't make the words come any more than she could make herself call the safeword. She was a failure.

He grabbed her arm when she damn near fell off the side of the table because she was shaking so badly. Her oiled feet slipped on the tiles. If not for his tightening grip on her arm, she'd have gone all the way down on her butt.

"Whoa, whoa," Anders said, his tone dropping into the realm of the soothing. "If you need to stop, we can call it right here, okay?"

"How about I fucking call it?"

Anna snapped around as Marcus came out of the crowd. He looked furious, and in her sky-rocketing panic, she didn't even notice that none of that fury was fixed on her.

Anders put up his hands, backing away from both her and the scene. "I'm done," he announced. "I came here to have a good time, not to get my ass beat."

"Clothes," Marcus told her.

She didn't need to be told twice. She fled back through the crowd, running on slippery feet all the way back to the bar where her things were still folded neatly, albeit on the floor by the couch where they'd been sitting. Another couple was there now.

"Excuse me." Humiliated beyond bearing, knowing this was all her fault, she couldn't even look at them. She scrambled into her dress, yanking her panties up and fumbling to get her shoes back on as fast as she could.

"Pony?"

Anna whipped around when she felt a timid tap on her

shoulder and bumped straight into Cynthia, knocking the full tray of drinks balanced on the shorter woman's arm to the floor. Everything broke.

"I'm sorry!" she blurted.

Oh God, and now here came Spencer, called forth from his office by the sound of shattering glasses.

"For fuck's sake, Cynthia," he snapped.

"I'm sorry!" Anna burst into tears, not noticing how he'd already stopped the instant he'd seen her face. "It was me! I'm sorry!"

She dropped to her knees, scrambling to grab the tray and as many of the broken pieces as she could find.

"Enough, girl." Spencer came at her.

"You'll cut yourself!" Cynthia dropped to her knees too, trying to catch Anna's wrists.

It was Marcus's voice that cut through the storm. "Anna, stop!"

The command froze her, and then cut her to ribbons. She had ruined everything. For Marcus, for Puppy. Anders. Everyone. She was worse than useless.

Ethen had been justified in shooting her.

"Anna." Reaching her side, Marcus grabbed her arm.

She was going to be sick.

Wrenching away from him, she bolted for the nearest bathroom. She barely made it before her rolling stomach rebelled. Nothing came up, but she heaved and gagged anyway. She was barely aware of when Marcus squeezed himself into the stall behind her, his strong arm wrapping around her waist as he gathered her hair out of the way. He held her over the toilet while she fell apart, and he didn't try to force her upright again until she was finally reduced to nothing but helpless spitting because her mouth wouldn't stop watering.

"I'm sorry," she cried.

He said nothing. He just drew her up into his arms, but his silence was damning. He was angry with her. He had to be. At the very least, he had to be disappointed.

She was disappointed in herself too. She'd failed at everything tonight.

The toilet in the stall beside them flushed. After a moment, a woman edged past their door, her wide eyes staring in at them before hurrying on out of the bathroom.

"We're going home," Marcus finally said.

"I'm sorry." She couldn't even bring herself to look at him.

"Stop apologizing."

Shoulders slumping, she let herself be pulled from the stall.

"Wash your face and rinse your mouth."

He followed her to the sink and she did as she was told, refusing to look at him even in the mirror.

"Let's go."

The command was terse, and it flayed her with all the things she knew she deserved to hear him say about how she'd behaved. And yet, angry as he was, he still opened the bathroom door for her.

"Leaving already?" Muscles called as Marcus pushed her on ahead of him, past the security desk with the heat of his hand burning into the small of her back.

Marcus didn't answer him. He simply opened that next door for her too, pushing her through it, out of the dungeon play area, through the locker room entry, and into the secret tunnel leading up and out.

"Please don't be mad at me," she begged, and before she could even turn around, he grabbed her. Suddenly, her back was to the brick wall and his hard body was against her front, pinning her to it.

His grip on her arms was almost painful it was so tight, but it was the look on his face that took her breath away. He sucked it straight from her lungs a bare heartbeat before he kissed her.

His mouth wasn't gentle. It was hard and fierce, plundering. And when he broke it, his rough voice was just as fierce when he told her, "It was not your fault, damn it. Stop apologizing." He shook her by the shoulders. "It was my fault, understand?"

Shocked as she was, she nodded, but she didn't understand at all. And she understood even less when his angry gaze dropped to her lips, sending shocks of raw awareness straight from them into her knotted stomach.

"It was my fault," Marcus said, "for letting you play with him. *My* fault for not vetting him better or stopping it sooner."

Was that his cock she could feel, digging hard into her belly where his hips held her pinned? She tried, but she couldn't catch her breath. She was panting, as if she'd just run a mile in less than a minute, but the only thing running right now was her heart. It raced, fast and unsteady. Even more unsteady than her knees.

Were he not holding her like this, she'd have collapsed at his feet, especially when he tore his gaze from her mouth and finally confessed, "I wasn't prepared to watch you play with another man."

He shook his head, correcting himself. "I don't want to watch you with other men, Anna. Ever." He shook her shoulders even more gently than before. "Do you understand?"

"Yes." She nodded, a bobblehead, unable to stop herself.

He looked at her mouth again, but the sparks were exploding inside her and this time the hunger was hers. She swooped up to catch his kiss halfway.

She yielded instantly, letting him take her, loving how swiftly his kiss deepened and his hunger for her grew until his kiss tasted angry all over again.

Letting go of her arms, he grabbed her ass, heaving her up until her feet left the floor. Latching onto his shoulders, she wrapped her legs around his hips, mewling into his mouth as he tore open his own pants first, and then at the skirt of her dress. He more ripped her panties aside than off, and in a single savage thrust, he was in her.

He drank the gasp from her lips, the air from her lungs. The soul from her body. The power of his thrusts scrubbed her back against the hard brick wall and washed her clean of every awful sensation from the failed scene that still haunted her. He didn't just banish Anders touch, he banished Ethen's.

"You're fucking mine," he growled into her mouth, bringing every waking nerve in her body joyously to life.

He drove her to come to the hard motions of his body and the demanding hunger of his mouth as he kissed the side of her neck, then bit and sucked hard. As if he wanted to mark her. Make her his. Only his. Just like he'd said.

Because he wanted her.

She cried out, ecstasy erupting. She hadn't meant to come, but he ripped it out of her. Marcus and his hard sucking mouth, ruthlessly raising that hickey on her neck in a place she hadn't a prayer of being able to cover.

Throwing back her head, she shouted as her body rebelled in the most excruciatingly pleasurable way.

He tore his mouth from her skin. "You just came without permission." The dark intensity of his eyes grew even darker with victory. "Good girl. *Good* girl, Anna!"

The pounding of his hips grew more forceful. His fingers dug into her ass as he redoubled his efforts, fucking her without restraint. She barely caught her breath before she was falling apart all over again.

"Good girl," he groaned, slamming into her and then stiffening sharply as he came too, grinding to get deeper, as if he couldn't get deep enough.

His body relaxed, but he didn't let her go.

She didn't let go of him either, not until her shaking legs betrayed her and she lost her grip around his waist.

He lowered her gently, keeping his hold on her until her feet touched the floor and her legs grew steady enough to support her.

"Y-your leg," she panted.

"I've got enough left in me," he growled back. "Talk about my leg again, and I'm going to have you back on that wall."

That was hardly a deterrent.

"Your leg," she said again, this time without stuttering. He arched a warning eyebrow, and she almost laughed.

There was a knock on the door just behind him. It cracked before Spencer's deeply disapproving voice stated, "I don't even let people I like do that out here. Find a fucking bed or take it somewhere else." The door swung closed on his not-so-quite mutter, "Now we have to sterilize the damn walls."

The door clicked shut.

Her legs were still shaking, not quite solid. Her pussy was tingling, aching in the best of ways. The look Marcus gave her then made both the aching and the shaking worse.

"I'm going to take you home, Anna."

For such a simple statement, all she could hear were the unmistakable layers inherent in the words he left unsaid.

Her pussy throbbed.

"But first—" He tipped his head. "—go back inside and see if the massage table you were just on is still available."

She swallowed the instant disappointment. He wasn't going to make her finish that scene with Anders, was he? "Why?"

"Because you're not leaving here, with that—" He thrust an accusing finger back at the door behind him, and the table where she'd scened, "—being what you remember most about your first night back at Black Light. Claim the table. I'll be along behind you."

He swatted the side of her ass to get her moving, then turned his attention to putting his cock back in his pants and fastening it up.

He was going to scene with her?

On the massage table?

Anna walked back into the dungeon as if she were in a dream. Her feet moved her, but she didn't notice anyone around her, the play stations they passed, or what was happening on them. All she knew was Marcus wasn't done touching her.

She could feel his hands on her already.

CHAPTER 12

Marcus

"I need to borrow a playbag," Marcus said, as he found Spencer making his rounds in the dungeon play area.

"You sullied my wall," Spencer replied, without looking around. "I touch that wall on my way in and out of here."

Stifling a sigh, Marcus refrained from rolling his eyes. "You do not. Nobody touches those walls."

"I might need to touch them. Someday. Klara might touch them."

He scoffed. "Talking to you when you're like this is like trying to reason with the worst princess brat mid-tantrum. I'm going to get you a tiara, I swear to God."

Spencer turned on him. "Says the unprepared dom who needs to borrow my playbag."

"Did you bring one or not?"

"It's in my office." Dismissing him, the club manager

turned his attention back to the goings on. "If I smell you on Klara's hand when she reaches for me later, I'm banning you both."

Snorting, Marcus started towards the office.

"Oh, and Marcus…"

Waving a hand, he kept walking. "I'll pay for the damn glasses. Just charge my account."

"Marcus."

Stopping misstep, he stifled another sigh and turned back. "Yes, my darling brat?"

Rolling his eyes, Spencer glared at him, then nodded in the other direction.

He followed the other man's gaze to where Anna was once more sitting on the massage table, waiting. She was fully clothed this time, one hand on her trim stomach as if willing her nerves to be still.

"Is she going to be okay?"

He intended to make sure of it. "Yes."

Eyeing him, Spencer finally nodded. "She looks good," he said. "Much better than the last time I saw her."

She looked better than good. To him, Marcus realized, she had become everything. Only more. More than a companion, or a submissive who lived in his house because someone had called in a favor. More than someone he had come to focus on more than the lingering pain in his bum leg. In fact, the only thing she wasn't, was a job.

How long had it been since he'd felt that way for someone?

"She is better," he agreed, his gaze softening as he watched her rub her palms against her skirted thighs, smoothing the fabric against her legs. She was nervous in a way she hadn't been when Anders had taken her off to scene.

Maybe because he mattered to her too, more than just some random dom at Black Light.

He couldn't remember the last time he'd had someone who had made him feel that special in a long time either.

"You've been good for her," Spencer said.

She'd been better for him.

"Congratulations."

Marcus nodded once. "Thanks for the bag."

"Rock her world."

Oh, he intended to.

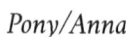

Pony/Anna

"CLOTHES OFF," Marcus announced, startling Anna. Nervous as she was, she hadn't noticed him making his way to her through the increasing crowd of club members, nor had she heard his approaching footsteps. She jumped a little when he set an unfamiliar play bag on the end of the table and a glass vase full of water and ice down on the floor.

There was no one else with him. Her heart skipped and that flock of butterflies in her stomach leapt and soared.

"Are... are you going to do it?" she asked as he opened the bag and rummaged through the contents.

Stopping, he looked at her a moment, then abandoned what he was doing and came around to where she was sitting. He braced a hand on the edge of the padded table to either side of her hips. "Let me be very clear. I am not prepared to watch you with anyone else. Now, I need you to be very clear with me. Do you want to play with someone else?"

No. God, no. Her one experience tonight had proved that. But how to tell him that? The words for something that deeply profound just didn't exist.

She shook her head.

"Let me be very clear about something else. I don't know if I will ever be able to watch you play with someone else. Does that scare you, make you happy, sad… nervous?"

"Relieved." The confession was out of her before she knew it was going to travel from her brain to her lips.

He nodded. "When I take you home tonight, I want to talk to you about renegotiating our contract. I'd like you to consider embarking on something less temporary than what currently exists between us. Is that something you want to do?"

She was going to cry all over again. She swallowed hard, blinking rapidly to cut back the tears, and nodded.

"If I have learned nothing else tonight, it's that my end goal has just become to put my collar on you. I meant what I said in the hall, Anna. I want you as mine, all of you. Every part. I want to own you—your mind, your body. All the parts you like, the parts you don't, the parts that still need work, everything. It'll take more than one conversation stretched out over many months, but be brutally honest with me. If you have reservations, we'll discuss them. If you have fears, we'll face them. If you need more time, I'll give it, as much as you need for as long as you need it. But if you know in your heart right now that being owned by me is something you don't want, I need you to tell me. You've been through hell, and I'll understand. But if you don't tell me no right now, I am going to claim every part of your body tonight, and I have no intention of sharing you. You. Will. Be. Mine. So, what do you want to do?"

She was shaking, she was so happy. "I want to take off my clothes."

"Do you understand that I intend to fuck your mouth tonight?"

She scrambled off the table in her haste to get on her

knees. She opened her mouth, the tears she'd been trying so hard to fight back overwhelming her to spill down her cheeks.

"I'm going to take your ass too."

She shoved far enough back from him to drop her head to the floor. Yanking her skirt up and her panties down, she thrust her ass into the air, grabbed her cheeks and spread them for him.

"Is that a yes?" He sounded amused.

"Yes, Sir," she said, loudly and clearly.

"I won't be gentle. Your body is going to feel my owner-ship every single day. You'll never have reason to doubt it."

She didn't know that being so thoroughly broken on someone else's words could be so beautiful. Letting go of her ass, she covered her face with both hands and just sobbed. "Thank you, Sir."

"Strip," he said again.

Scrubbing at her watery eyes, she crawled to her feet and stripped out of her dress. A milky stain coated the gusset of her panties, proof of his ownership of her pussy already. She wadded them up, embarrassed, proud, and flustered all at once.

He held out his hand before she could stuff them under her discarded dress. Reluctantly, she handed them over, help-less to do anything but watch as he turned them crotch out.

"Get used to this," he told her. "I'll be using you often and well."

Shivers wracked her. She loved that terminology. She loved the instant visualization it inspired, and knowing he meant exactly what he said.

"Up on the table. Face down." He held out a steadying hand until she was up and then went back to his bag. She heard the light click of bondage rings bumping against wood and hard plastic. She resisted the urge to look back over her shoulder, though the urge did get stronger when she heard the softer tell-tale clink of ice knocking about in a glass.

"Have you ever tried fire writing?" he asked.

She shook her head. She'd seen it a few times, but never participated.

"Temperature and sensation play?"

She shook her head again. "Some. Not a lot."

"It's not painful, although the heat can be both pleasurable and intense, depending on your skin sensitivity and how I choose to do it."

She heard the telltale clink of ice rattling in the vase as he shook it gently. Tiny drops of cold water sprinkled her back and she jerked, rolling halfway over in her haste to look back. What she hadn't noticed before was, inside the vase, immersed in lots of ice cubes and water, were two glass dildoes—one blue and one clear.

"Just so you know," he said, "these were brand new and in their original boxes, and I'm pretty sure I just paid twice what Spencer did for them. I also intend to make this very intense, but I promise you won't get hurt. Do you think you can trust me to keep that promise?"

That was an insane question to ask after she'd just offered him both her mouth and her ass, her whole body after tonight, she suddenly realized. "Yes, Sir."

He patted her hip. "Get comfortable while I set up."

She pillowed her head on her arms while he pulled up a portable table and laid out the cup of ice he'd brought, a bottle of hair mousse, personal lubricant, long strips of cotton, towels, and a bottle of rubbing alcohol. Pouring the alcohol into another cup, he dropped two buttons into it, white cotton-wrapped tips down, and doused them. He lit a candle, and was ready. The light caress of his hand moving over her back told her he was about to start.

With the fire, the ice, or his hand? She didn't know, but she was giddy to find out. This was what she'd missed feeling the first time she was on this table tonight.

"Let's get you ready."

His broad hand pushed between her legs, not cupping her pussy, but slipping into the wetness he'd already built there. The unexpectedness of it startled her, but the pleasure of his penetrating fingers as he pushed first two, and then three, up inside her made every nerve he stroked come instantly back to life.

"Nice and wet."

The huskiness in his voice melted her, right up until his fingers pulled out in favor of giving her pussy a brisk patting spank. He ended the gentle assault with a soothing rub that wrung a soft moan from her.

He shifted his focus, his touch finding the bud of her back passage. He circled with the flat of his fingers, applying steady pressure while her rebel muscles tightened and tightened. Stopping just shy of invading her there, he said, "But this... this is bone dry, and that just won't do. Will it, Anna?"

She could barely think. Was that rhetorical or did he want her to answer him?

He smacked her bottom, and she almost came up off the table at the sharpness of the sting.

"No, Sir," she blurted.

"No, sir," he echoed, his light-hearted humor a stark contrast to the severity of that swat. Taking the lube off the table, he popped the top and drizzled a generous dollop into the crack of her ass. "We'll do this part now. I wouldn't want to forget in the heat of the moment and accidentally fuck you dry."

His fingers found the drops of lube sliding down between her cheeks and returned the slickness where it was needed.

She buried her face in her arms as he applied gentle pressure again, gradually forcing the ring of reluctant muscle to open.

"Have you been fucked up the ass?"

"Yes," she groaned, trying to hold as still as possible as a single digit worked its way in. He didn't penetrate far, but it was enough to send a twinge of discomfort through her. She gritted her teeth, trying to breathe through it.

"How long has it been?" Wrapping his arm around her hip, he worked his free hand under her in search of her pussy.

"A long time." Her breath caught when he brushed her clit, and her hips twitched as he pinched it.

"I'm not going to neglect any part of you," he vowed, his finger beginning that mortifying dance, sinking in and out of her in slow fucking motions until the twinge of discomfort melted away, and all she was left with was the breathtaking magic of his ownership. "However, I promise I'll find ways to help you enjoy all or most of it."

He invaded deeper, the fingers of his other hand caressing her clit until the pinch of returning discomfort faded away again. "Two fingers now."

She grabbed the end of the table, her legs beginning to shake as the single digit withdrew and two began to work their way in.

"Oh." She groaned through gritted teeth. Too full. Too much. Though she fought to relax, her muscles tightened to keep him out. Tensing only made it hurt worse and she had plenty of experience in just how bad it could be. Yet, when the ring of muscle at last gave way and he sank his fingers into her, the worst of the pain was more like an orgasm, wrung from her courtesy of the swift rubbing circles assaulting her clit. The groan became a throaty moan.

"Do you like having my fingers in your ass, Anna? Because that sounds as if you do."

She nearly came off the table when he pinched her clit, the

fingers of his other hand twisting sideways inside her. She bit the back of her hand, her hips writhing, needing a return to the rubbing he'd just ceased.

Abandoning her pussy altogether, he released her waist and sharply slapped her bottom. Two crisp swats now, one for each of the fingers he was now pumping in and out of her ass in hard fucking motions.

"Yes!" she shouted. "Yes, Sir, I like it! Please—oh!"

He took his hands from her entirely. "Too late. When I ask a question, I expect a prompt response. We've had this discussion before."

She expected him to spank her, but he didn't. A handful of wet ice cubes dropped onto her back instead, shocking the pleasure right out of her. She sucked a sharp gasp, but his hand flattened on the small of her back, pinning her to the table.

"Oh my God!"

Cold was not her friend, no matter how wildly her pussy now pulsed and throbbed. Her nails raked the table's edge, her body fighting not to squirm as he stroked the ice cubs down her back. Cold caressed her from shoulders to ass, the melting ice sending rivulets of water tickling down her curves.

"Do I need to tie you down?"

Leaving the ice to melt in the small of her back, he dipped another cube out of the vase. This he tucked into the crack of her ass, wedging it directly over her anus to melt and dibble cold water into the folds of her eagerly twitching pussy.

"You're still not answering me. I wonder why." He dipped out another cube, this one finding its maddening way to the sensitive back of her thigh. "Is it because you find it embarrassing to admit in public that you want the things I'm making you say?"

"N-no, Sir!" Giddy goosebumps prickled her. She'd wanted the things he was doing to her for so long. What had it been

186

now, just a few short weeks ago that she'd have given anything and everything just to be touched? Well, he was touching her now and the cold sitting stationary in the small of her back and between her ass cheeks was killing her. "Please?"

"Please, what?" he returned, scooping out a few ice cubes more and laying them on the back of her thigh. Covering them with his hand, he stroked the length of her leg.

It was all she could do not to kick or roll over.

"I said, do you want me to tie you down?"

"N-no, Sir!" Her pussy spasmed hard, a rolling wave of orgasmic shivers that shot to her stiffening nipples and then to her womb. Melting water trickled over her sides and over her pussy. Her outer folds were so cold and yet her clit pulsed hot. She couldn't speak. She couldn't think. If she opened her mouth now, all that would come out would be squeaks as she writhed, helplessly wanting to both escape and not.

"Hold still, please." He circled the back of her knee once before journeying on toward her feet.

"I—I can't!"

"No?" The clink of tinkling ice announced his return to the vase. A half second later, the heat of his hand cupped her pussy, parting the chilled folds.

She arched sharply, losing what little composure she had to shout as the tip of the first chilled dildo pushed inside her. "Oh my God!"

"How about now?" he asked, mercilessly pushing the dildo deeper until the cold of it was all the way up inside her. "Can you hold still for me now?"

She couldn't even breathe. She was shaking, the cold seeping in deeper than just her skin now. It was in her muscles, in her core. Her nipples were so tight and hard they hurt. Locking her jaw to keep her teeth from chattering, she buried her face in the table padding, but there was no escape.

"Are you cold?" He pumped the dildo slowly in and out of her. "Shall I warm you, honey?"

Groaning through gritted teeth, she already knew a comfortable blanket was not at all what he meant. Was he going to use the flash cotton now, the candle, a spanking? As cold as her ass was right now, even light swats from his hard hands would be quickly unbearable.

"You really are ignoring me."

"No!" she squeaked, but already he was back at the vase and the lightly clinking ice sent ominous shivers racing down her spine. She braced for cold, more ice dumped onto her back or wedged between her ass cheeks to replace the cube that had melted away to nothing. What she wasn't braced for, was the trickling line of hot wax that suddenly poured the length of her spine from midway down her back all the way to the hills of her buttocks. He used all the liquid wax he could coax from the candle, dripping circles over each nether cheek in turn while she grunted and ground into the table padding.

The heat stung everywhere it hit cold, her flesh erupting into tingling, burning chills. Her nerves couldn't process it. Neither could her brain, and her ass humped the table, bouncing and writhing in an effort to evade. The wax hardened almost instantly. He caressed the ridge as it hardened on her skin, then cupped her bottom and prized her open.

She'd never heard him put the candle aside or pick up the second dildo. All she felt was that half-second of erotic terror as the cold glass head nudged unerringly in search of her anal rim.

"Do you want me to fuck your asshole?"

No! Yes! Please? She did and she didn't, and she didn't know.

"Fuck!"

Marcus chuckled, soft and low. "Close enough."

It pushed into her.

Cold, *cold*, COLD!

Her bowels clamped down, but he was stronger and in the dildo went, shivering her so deeply.

"Roll over, but carefully. If the dildos come out, I'll find someone in this place willing to loan me a cane and you will be one very sorry little girl before I'm done."

Shivering, she carefully rolled onto her back and lay down flat, with two inflexible cocks shoved up into her frozen insides. Her tender back ached everywhere the heat had seared her.

"Look at those pretty little nipples."

She didn't need to look. They were hard as diamonds and every bit as desperate as her needy pussy.

"Are you cold?" Once more searching her folds until he found her clit, the heat of his fingertips soon had her moaning and squirming again. "Let's see if we can warm you back up."

She was so close to coming, despite her shaking and shivering. When he took his hand away, she actually grabbed after his arm.

Just as quickly, he caught her nipples, giving the hard beads a disciplinary pinch. She arched, her back coming up off the table. The glass base of the dildo in her ass bumped into the padding beneath her, pushing it deeper. "Don't do that again. You think this is difficult to take? I'm doing this for pleasure. Don't make me turn it into a punishment."

A hot rush of arousal flooded her pussy, a crazy reaction that was at complete odds with the riot going on in the rest of her.

"Do you want this to be a punishment?" He tweaked her nipples harder, and her hips took on a life of their own, grinding to make the dildo move. Her breath caught, her throat tightening to keep back another moan.

Letting go, he captured a fistful of her hair instead and wrenched her head back, forcing her to meet his stare.

"Do you," he repeated, softly, dangerously, every nuance charged with an eroticism that made the walls of her core contract on the pseudo cock inside her, "want me to punish you?"

No. Never.

"Yes," she whimpered.

He tipped his head. The corners of his mouth curled into a smile as he reached down between her legs to take hold of the glass cock in her pussy. She knew she was every bit as wet as she suspected when he stopped, glanced down, and then knowingly locked eyes with her again.

He tsked. "Naughty, naughty, girl. I was going to fuck you with this." He pumped the dildo, and all she could feel was the cold and the fullness of having two cocks hitting all the right spots as he thrust. "Now I think I need to do something else."

He plucked the one from her pussy, robbing her of that blessed fullness and dropped the dildo back in the ice water.

Her arousal was unbearable. So was her fear that he would pour the icy water from the vase all over her, but he picked up the batons instead, plucking them from the glass where they had absorbed the alcohol. His warm hand caressed up her torso from her mons, to her breasts, and finally her neck.

She had no personal experience with fire writing, but seeing him with the batons in his hand didn't frighten her. The ease with which he had them tucked between his first and last fingers, the alcohol-soaked swabs positioned as far as possible apart, said he had more than enough experience to keep her safe.

He lit the first swab on the candle, and the palm of his other hand swept another wandering path over her breasts and belly, caressing the canvas he was about to paint.

Through the ice, she had been so distracted by the cold that she hadn't noticed the crowd that was gathering, but she noticed them now. Shadowy figures jockeyed for the best vintages from which to watch as he lowered the unlit swap to tap her nipple. The pungent smell of alcohol and the coolness of the damp on her breast was grounding, but only until he flipped his hand and tapped the lit baton to the same spot. Heat and flame ignited on her nipple a heartbeat before he brushed it out with his open hand.

He paused, smile softening as he looked at her. "Was that terrible?"

"No, Sir."

"Where are you at?"

"Green," she answered, staring in wonder at her breast. It hadn't hurt. Not even a little. She'd barely even felt the heat.

Flipping to the unlit baton, he snaked an invisible 's' in rubbing alcohol between her breasts, then lit it. Racing flames followed the pattern he'd drawn before he brushed it out again. This time the heat stayed in her skin, a sharp contrast to the cold of her back and the icy pool her ass was in.

It was pretty. It was warm too, but again it didn't burn, and once the flame was out, the only sensation that lingered was a faint tingling that might have been nothing more than her hyper awareness of his caressing hand in all the nerves eager for it beneath her skin.

"Still green?" he asked.

She nodded.

"All right, let's get down to business."

Her heart fluttered as she watched him draw a jagged bolt of lightning down her stomach, and set it aflame. Her stomach was more sensitive than her breasts, the heat stung even after he'd brushed it out, although only as badly as the snap of a rubber band.

He drew the straight line of an arrow pointing unerring down to her mons and her back arched as the heat got stronger when he set it on fire, not once, but three times. He brushed out each new flame before lighting her up again,

191

drawing squiggles down her thighs, setting the tops of each foot briefly on fire, and then returning to her chest to do the same for each breast. Turning, he extinguished the burning baton and dropped them both on the small table, then selected the newly chilled dildo once more.

She groaned as he let the excess water drip onto her breasts and belly. The shock of cold where she had just been so warm was a hell in and of itself. It felt beautiful, especially in the places he'd set on fire more than once, leaving her skin as sensitive as if she'd been mildly sunburned.

"Spread your legs."

She hadn't realized she'd pulled them closed. Knowing how cold it was going to be, she grabbed the table with both hands and obeyed.

"Ah!" If anything, it was even colder than before. She felt fuller too, stretched to accept not a slow penetrating thrust, but motions that were harder now. Deeper and more demanding. Conquering. Claiming her pussy with a cock that felt more like an icicle.

"No!"

Except no wasn't what she meant at all.

"Color?" he demanded.

"Green!"

He spanked her mons, punishing her tender clit, and fucked her harder.

"Noo-oo!" She covered her traitorous mouth with both hands, but he spread her folds with his fingers and bent, capturing her clit in the overwhelming heat of his mouth. "God!"

He devoured her, lashing and licking without mercy, nibbling with his lips and even gently his teeth. He had her on the verge of wildness. She nearly climbed the length of the table before he pinned her down. Hooking the bases of both dildoes, he held them the same way he'd done the batons and fucked her with both at once.

He wouldn't tell her to come, but oh how she wanted him to. She wanted to yield that control and gift him with the impending result.

"Please!" she wailed.

He stopped, slapping her pussy and rubbing hard before taking his hand away. "On your belly. Don't lose the dildoes."

That was easier said than done. She was so wet now and her pussy was clenching rhythmically, needing the orgasm he'd just denied her. She'd also squirmed so far up the table that her head was almost hanging off it. She tried to scoot down, but he stopped her. He picked up the flash cotton and the feather soft brush of it trailed down her back. He lay two paths over the summits of both ass cheeks, all the way down onto the backs of her thighs to the infamous sit spots.

"Don't move," he told her. "No matter what, don't move. It's going to be intense. Can you handle it?"

She nodded.

"Are you ready?"

She nodded again, but everything was concentrated on the hard cold cocks inside her and her desperation for him to start fucking her again. Right up until he came around to the head of the table and unbuckled his pants.

"Open," he ordered.

She lunged the instant his cock came into view. His grip on her hair was the cake, but his cum would be the icing and she swallowed as much of him as she could get into her mouth.

Could she drive him as crazy as he'd made her? She didn't know, but she was determined to find out. Only he was almost too much. He hit the back of her throat, tripping gag reflexes she'd thought she'd tamed a long time ago. He didn't withdraw, but cupped the back of her head, steadily choking her until the tears were pouring down her face and the lack of air made stars burst in her eyes. He pulled out, letting her suck and gasp for air, before forcing his way back into her mouth and starting all over again.

She was not in control. Not even just a little, and her pussy loved it.

She never saw it when he picked up the candle, but she heard the sizzling flash of ignition and felt the searing heat suddenly race down her back, ignite on her ass, and snap across the backs of her tender thighs with all the focused intensity of a cane strike.

She'd have shouted if not for his cock in her throat. She'd have jumped up too, but his hand on the back of her head held her down.

It was just a flash and done, but the lingering sting of that searing heat remained, flaring hotter the way spankings so often did, before just as swiftly dying back to nothing but a tingle.

Releasing her head, he pulled out of her mouth. Before she could catch her breath, he had the glass cock ripped from her body and was up on the table with her.

She tried to get her knees under her, but he swatted her bottom and straddled her thighs. The hard jab of his prodding cock nudged against her ass as she grabbed the table.

Yanking her head back with her own hair, he said hot against her ear, "Take it and cum."

He shoved, and she did, shouting as she came.

He broke her, but he did it beautifully. Savagely. 'Bum' leg or not. Claiming this last part of her like exactly what he was, the man she now belonged to.

A man worth having.

A man who truly wanted her.

EPILOGUE

"*W*hat if it didn't work?" Anna fretted, sitting on the courthouse bench outside the courtroom her case had been assigned to. She wasn't just nervous. She was beyond nervous. "What if nothing I said mattered?"

Sitting next to her, Marcus was the epitome of relaxation as he waited for the attorneys to emerge and announce the outcome. "What did I say the last six times you asked that?"

She couldn't remember.

No, that wasn't true. She remembered, she just didn't like the answer.

"That we'll cross that bridge when we get to it." She buried her face in both hands.

Her meeting with the judge had been, hands down, the scariest moment of her life. She was seventeen whole pounds heavier and healthier than the hospital records showed. She'd started seeing a real, licensed therapist—one Dr. Madeline Parrish, another Black Light member who was far easier to talk to than Anna ever would have imagined. She was dressing herself, and had even managed a shopping trip without hyperventilating. Marcus assured her she was a lot more confident, too, although she didn't always agree with that assessment. All week long, she'd felt as if she were marching toward this moment through a field full of landmines.

It had been almost an hour since the judge had pulled her into his private chambers. What if she'd said the wrong things to him... looked nervous at the wrong time... done something that made him think her responses were scripted— because she and Marcus *had* practiced for this. What if she lost?

Would they make her move out of Marcus's house? Would she have to take her collar off for good, and not just for the duration of time she was spending now in the courthouse? Would they let her get her collar out of the glove box in his car before they took her away?

That she could lose not only her freedom but Marcus too, was real. And it was terrifying.

"Want to go for a walk on the beach?" Marcus asked, a font of infinite patience... at least when his Dom buttons weren't being pushed.

Dropping her hands back into her lap, she sighed and settled back on the bench. She wasn't sure even meditation was going to help today, but she closed her eyes and tried to relax.

"We're walking side by side on a white sandy beach," he began, his broad fingers brushing hers as he took her hand in his. "The sun is warm on our shoulders. A comfortable wind plays in your beautiful blonde hair, and your hand is in mine. You feel warm, and safe. Because you'll never be anything else when you're with me."

Her eyes opening, her nervous heart now pounding in her chest for a completely different reason, Anna looked at him.

"Do you know I love you?" he asked softly. Not that it mattered. Courthouses were made to echo and everyone sitting in on the benches in this hall couldn't help but over-hear him, not that he seemed to care. "Do you, Anna?"

She nodded, tiny quick jerks of her head. "Yes. I love you too. I do."

"You know what happens when you say that to a man who feels this deeply about you?"

Her heart was hammering in her throat. She shook her head.

Leaning sideways towards her, Marcus lowered his voice for her and her alone. "He stays with you for the rest of his life."

Anna breathed in, what felt like the first breath she'd taken all day long. She opened her mouth, but stopped when the door to the courtroom beside them opened and out stepped her lawyer.

"Congratulations," he said with a grin, and if he said anything else after that, she didn't hear it.

All the fear, all the stress, all the worst 'what ifs' that her treacherous brain could come up with—none of it mattered. Letting out a shriek of pure joy, Anna threw herself into Marcus's arms.

She had won. She was going to be allowed to take care of herself.

And the best part was, she already knew she wasn't going to have to.

"Want to go out to celebrate?" Marcus asked, but going out was the last thing she wanted right now.

Grinning, so happy she could almost cry, she shook her head. "I want to go home." To the home she'd never again have to worry that she'd be forced to leave; with a man she loved and who not only loved her back, but who wanted her. "And fair warning, Marcus, the minute I get you there, I am going to knock you on your back and ravish you completely."

"You think so?" Marcus replied, but that by now familiar

spark was both lighting his eyes and darkening his smile. She loved it when he looked at her like this.

"I know so."

His arms tightened around her waist, drawing her in that much closer. "Good girl," he chuckled, and he probably would have kissed her.

If only she hadn't kissed him first.

The End

THERE ARE plenty more **Black Light** stories coming! Next up is **Black Light: Worthy** by new Black Collar Press author, Stella Moore. Check out chapter one for an early taste.

***

Favoring his right knee, Austin Barrick limped his way through the crowded locker room and lowered himself onto a bench with a grunt. It was the only verbal acknowledgment of the pain shooting up his leg he allowed himself.

He was getting too fucking old for this.

At thirty-two, most people were just getting into the swing of things, career-wise. But he was racing head-on towards retirement and he knew it. What was worse, the rest of the team knew it. It was impossible to miss the sideways glances of the rookies and the sympathetic smiles of the more seasoned players.

A pair of naked, hairy legs appeared in his peripheral vision as he worked at a knot in his neck. "You okay there, Barrick?"

Tony Fucking Torres. The Washington National's newest shining star. Brand new recruit from the University of Michigan, and still young enough for a smattering of pimples along his otherwise perfect jawline.

And, although nobody had come right out and said it yet, Austin's replacement.

Without looking up, Austin waved a hand, dismissing his young protegé. "I'm fine. Just a headache from listening to you hens clucking all damn day."

Grumbling and laughter filled the locker room, but the legs didn't move. "You sure you're okay, man? I thought I saw you limping."

Finally lifting his head, Austin peeled his lip back in a sneer. "Sorry to disappoint you, kid. But you ain't getting rid of me that easy."

Ignoring the twinge of guilt at the hurt on the younger man's face, Austin made his way to the shower, forcing himself not to limp. Which meant his knee was screaming at him by the time he'd showered and dressed for his meeting with the new financial planner his agent had pushed on him. Apparently, this chick was the cream of the crop when it came to investments and shit, and it had taken some serious fast-talking to get her to even accept a meeting with him.

Obviously not a baseball fan if she wasn't falling all over herself for a chance at Austin Barrick's finances.

Most of the team had dispersed by the time he made it to the parking lot, so he allowed himself a slight limp on his way to the monstrous SUV that had been his first big purchase when he'd signed with Chicago ten years ago. He could afford a dozen just like it every year with his current contract with the Hawks, but he was loath to part with his first.

The money chick's office was nearly an hour drive with traffic, and his mood hadn't improved any by the time he found a spot at the far end of the parking lot and limped his way to the shiny glass building. "At least there's a fucking elevator," he mumbled to himself as he punched the button for the tenth floor.

The elevator in question zipped up to the requested floors

almost silently, and the doors opened to reveal a wall of windows with *Katherine Callahan, CFP* printed on the spotless glass doors.

A severe-looking older woman with her silver hair clipped back in a bun from which not even a single hair dared to escape, glanced up from her computer when he opened the door. "Do you have an appointment?"

"Yeah. Barrick."

The woman's gaze flicked downward, and her unpainted lips came together in a time-honored expression of disapproval. "You are fifteen minutes late, Mr. Barrick."

"Sorry about that," he glanced at the name plate on the sleek metal desk, "Donna." Despite his irritation at not just being late but being called on it, he flashed her a grin. "Traffic, parking, all that jazz."

"Ms. Callahan has a very tight schedule."

Gritting his teeth behind the smile, he nodded. "Understood. Won't happen again."

With a noncommittal hum, Donna stood and rounded the desk. "Follow me." Sturdy, practical heels clicking on the tile, she led him down a short hallway to a corner office and gave a quick, brisk knock on the closed door.

"Mr. Barrick is here for your four o'clock," she announced, opening the door to a huge, sparsely decorated office.

Austin followed her inside, expecting a similar version of the gatekeeper. But the woman behind the desk nearly had his tongue rolling out of his mouth when she stood to greet him.

Hair so dark it was nearly black fell in sleek waves over her shoulders, brushing against the swell of breasts she'd tried to hide behind the perfectly cut business suit. Lush, full curves instantly filled his imagination with visions of her bent over the polished wood of her desk, welts covering her gorgeously round ass as he gripped her hips and pounded into her.

Giving himself a mental shake, he stepped forward and

stretched out a hand. "You can call me Austin. Katherine, right?"

Pale pink lips turned up in a polite, professional smile and almond-shaped eyes met his as she accepted the handshake, but there was no warmth in the brown depths. "Pleased to meet you, Mr. Barrick." She held out her unoccupied hand and the efficient Donna placed a thick, white folder in her palm. "Thank you, Donna. Would you bring us some ice water, please?"

Jesus, the woman was as cold as the refreshments she'd just requested. "Thanks, Katie." It was petty and rude, but the snotty way she'd called him *Mr. Barrick* had gotten under his skin.

If she'd been ice before, her voice turned glacial at the nickname. "Katherine or Ms. Callahan, please."

What did it say about him that the clipped, cold tones just made him all the more eager to see her splayed out on her desk for him? He imagined miss prim and proper Katherine Callahan would be utterly embarrassed by the images running rampant through his imagination. Then again, maybe a little humiliation was just what she needed. In his experience, it went a long way toward helping stubborn little subbies learn their place.

Even if she wasn't a submissive - and wouldn't that be a damn shame - he couldn't seem to keep his brain from conjuring up an image of what she would look like with an embarrassed flush covering her entire luscious body. His foul mood vanished as his imagination went into overdrive.

"Katherine," he conceded, pushing aside his bad mood and turning up the charm with an apologetic smile.

"Thank you." Taking her seat, she opened the file Donna had handed her. When she gestured to the guest chair, he sat with a silent prayer of gratitude for the opportunity to stretch out his knee.

"I had your agent send over your current portfolio," she began, her eyes glancing down to scan the contents of the file he had a sneaking suspicion she already knew by heart. It was a power play, meant to let him know she didn't consider him any more important than any other client. And he couldn't help but respect the hell out of it. No doubt she had more than one client who needed to be knocked down a peg or two on a regular basis.

"And?" he prompted when she paused.

"It's not bad." Flipping the file closed, she looked up, her lips curving up in a fierce, damn near predatory smile. "I can do a hell of a lot better."

"You don't need to sell yourself to me. Mary said you're the best, so you're the best."

"I appreciate the vote of confidence. Would you like me to explain what I have in mind?"

"Sure." Not that he'd understand a single word of it. He just liked listening to her talk. She had a voice like good whiskey: smooth with a hint of a bite.

"To start with, you're a little stock-heavy at the moment. Which was a good move at the beginning of your career, when you could reasonably expect a steady income for a while. You've had decent growth the past few years, so now I'd like to look at preserving your current capital."

The implication pricked at his pride - and his temper. "I'm not retiring."

She raised a single, perfectly sculpted eyebrow in his direction. "I didn't say you were. But you will be, and relatively soon, all things considered."

Leaning forward in his chair, he jabbed a finger at her from across the desk. "I've got a good five years left in me, at least." Maybe. If his goddamn knee would cooperate.

"Which, in the world of financial planning, is relatively soon," she replied without so much as blinking. Turning to face him more fully, she folded her hands on top of the file and pinned him with that ice-queen stare. "You may be a big shot out on the field, Mr. Barrick. But in here, I'm the all-star. You can either listen to me and I can give you a nice, comfortable life once you are inevitably forced out, or you can take your money and your business elsewhere. I have neither the time nor the patience for clients who throw hissy fits in my office."

If she hadn't had a damn good point, he might have walked out then and there. But she was right, and he was wrong, and he was man enough to admit it. Leaning back again, he flashed her another smile. "Fair enough. In here, you're the boss." Points to her for not so much as blinking when he deliberately emphasized *in here*.

Instead, she just inclined her head and gave him a polite, "Thank you."

Donna chose that moment to return with a small silver tray ladened with a pale blue pitcher and two matching glasses. She silently poured water into one of the glasses and placed it on a coaster in front of her boss before offering him the second glass.

"Thanks," he said, toasting her with the tumbler. Apparently, the two women were cut from the same cloth as Donna barely acknowledged him.

"Do you need anything else, Ms. Callahan?"

"No, that's all for now. Thank you, Donna." Katherine took a sip of her water as her assistant slipped silently out of the room. "All right, Mr. Barrick. Where were we?"

The desire to see if he could ruffle her won out over any desire to hear more about stocks and bonds and whatever the hell else she wanted to talk about. "You were about to agree to have dinner with me."

It worked. For the first time since he'd walked into the office, she looked flustered. Pink crept up her neck from under the collar of her stuffy business suit and her eyes widened slightly. "I'm sorry?"

"What are you apologizing for?"

The color on her neck rushed to her cheeks. "I wasn't. You -" She took a deep, deliberate breath, and he tried valiantly to ignore the way her breasts rose and fell beneath the curve-hugging blazer. "We never discussed meeting outside the office, Mr. Barrick."

"Then let's discuss it now. What are you doing tonight, Katherine?"

"Working."

"Come on. Even a woman as dedicated as you has to eat sometime, right?"

"I - well - yes. I suppose." Little wrinkles of confusion appeared along her brow, delighting him in a perverse way. Throwing her off balance was the most fun he'd had with a woman in years, in or out of the bedroom. Even the eager submissives at Black Light hadn't captivated him the way she had in the past few minutes.

"Then eat with me. We'll go wherever you want. We can talk money or whatever makes you happy that isn't turning great big piles of cash into bigger piles of cash."

A polite smile, bordering on patronizing, curved her lips. "I'm not that interesting, Mr. Barrick. I'm afraid you'll be bored to death."

"I highly doubt that. Dinner with a smart, gorgeous woman? What could possibly be boring about that?"

She pulled her bottom lip between her teeth, worrying at her perfectly applied lipstick before she caved with a quiet sigh. "All right. But just dinner, and just this once. I don't date clients, Mr. Barrick. It's -"

"Taboo?" he interrupted with an exaggerated wiggle of his eyebrows. "Sexy?"

"Highly inappropriate."

Grinning, he placed his elbows on the desk and leaned in. "Baby, you're about to find out that highly inappropriate is my favorite way to do things."

"I hate to tell you this, Mr. Barrick, but that isn't exactly a state secret."

The dry, sarcastic retort had him blinking in surprise before he snorted out a laugh. "See? Gorgeous, smart, *and* funny. You just keep adding to the deal here, Ms. Callahan. I don't see myself getting bored any time soon."

"If you say so. I have some things to wrap up here and then I'll meet you downstairs."

"Works for me. And you can figure out where you'd like to eat, too. I'm up for," he deliberately let his gaze drift from her face to her spectacular breasts and back up again, "anything."

Snagging one of her business cards from the display on her desk, he scribbled his number on the back. "Text me when you're ready and I'll meet you out front."

Grab your copy of **Black Light: Worthy** by Black Collar Press author, Stella Moore.

ABOUT THE AUTHOR

Fortunate enough to live with my Daddy Dom, I am a Little, coffee whore, pain slut, administrator at two of my local BDSM dungeons, resident of the wilds of freakin' Kansas (still don't know how I ended up here) and submissive to the love of my life. An International and USA Bestselling Author, I have penned more than 150 novels, novellas and short stories, and am the author of the Masters of the Castle series.

I also write under the names of Denise Hall, Darla Phelps, and Penny Alley.

CONNECT WITH HER

Visit Maren Smith's blog here:
http://badgirlscorner.blog

ALSO BY MAREN SMITH

Black Light Releases:

Shameless (Black Light: Roulette Redux, Book 7)

Black Light: Fearless by Maren Smith

Black Light: Celebrity Roulette by Various Authors

Black Light: Brave by Maren Smith

Black Light: Wanted by Maren Smith

The Red Petticoat Saloon Series:

Jade's Dragon

Warming Emerald

Masters of the Castle Series:

Book 1, Holding Hannah

Book 2, Kaylee's Keeper

Book 3, Saving Sara

Book 4, Sweet Sinclair

Book 5, Chasing Chelsea

Book 6, Owning O

Book 7, Maddy Mine

Book 8, Seducing Sandy

Witness Protection Program Box Set

Corbin's Bend:

Last Dance for Cadence (Season 1, Book 8)

Have Paddle, Will Travel (Season 2, Book 7)

A Few Other Titles:

B-Flick

Build-A-Daddy

The Great Prank

Jinxie's Orchids

Life After Rachel

The Locket

The Mountain Man

Real

Something Has To Give

GET A FREE BLACK LIGHT BOOK

Enjoy your trip to Black Light? There's a lot more sexy fun to be had. All of the books in the series can be read as standalone stories and can also be enjoyed in any reading order.

Get started with a FREE copy of **Black Light: Rocked** today. Your fun doesn't need to end yet!

BLACK COLLAR PRESS

Black Collar Press is a small publishing house started by authors Livia Grant and Jennifer Bene in late 2016. The purpose was simple - to create a place where the erotic, kinky, and exciting worlds they love to explore could thrive and be joined by other like-minded authors.

If this is something that interests you, please go to the Black Collar Press website and read through the FAQs. If your questions are not answered there, please contact us directly at: blackcollarpress@gmail.com

WHERE TO FIND BLACK COLLAR PRESS:

- Newsletter: http://bit.ly/2JY23Wi
- Website: http://www.blackcollarpress.com/
- Facebook: https://www.facebook.com/blackcollarpress/
- Twitter: https://twitter.com/BlackCollarPres
- Black Light East and West may be fictitious, but you can now join our very real Facebook Group for Black Light Fans - Black Light Central

BLACK LIGHT SERIES

Did you enjoy your visit to Black Light? Have you read the other books in the series? They can all be enjoyed as stand-alone books read in any order.

Season One

Infamous Love, A Black Light Prequel by Livia Grant
Black Light: Rocked by Livia Grant
Black Light: Exposed by Jennifer Bene
Black Light: Valentine Roulette by Various Authors
Black Light: Suspended by Maggie Ryan
Black Light: Cuffed by Measha Stone
Black Light: Rescued by Livia Grant

Season Two
Black Light: Roulette Redux by Various Authors
Complicated Love, A Black Light Novel by Livia Grant
Black Light: Suspicion by Measha Stone
Black Light: Obsessed by Dani René

Black Light: Fearless by Maren Smith
Black Light: Possession by LK Shaw

Season Three
Black Light: Celebrity Roulette by Various Authors
Black Light: Purged by Livia Grant
Black Light: Defended by Golden Angel
Black Light: Scandalized by Livia Grant
Black Light: Charmed by Jennifer Bene

Season Four
Black Light: Roulette War by Various Authors
Black Light: Brave by Maren Smith
Black Light: Unbound by Jennifer Bene and Lesley Clark
Black Light: Branded by Kay Elle Parker

Season Five
Black Light: Roulette Rematch by Various Authors
Black Light: Bred by Shane Starrett
Black Light: Wanted by Maren Smith
Black Light: Worthy by Stella Moore
Black Light: Saved by Raisa Greywood

Season Six
Black Light: The Menagerie by Maren Smith
Infamous Trio Boxed Set by Livia Grant
Black Light: Cured by Vivian Murdoch
Black Light: Disciplined by Livia Grant (Fall 2022)
Black Light: Protocol by Shane Starrett (Fall 2022)
Black Light: Secret by Samantha A. Cole (Fall 2022)
And many more planned!

Season Seven

Black Light: Gamble by Livia Grant (Early 2023)

Black Light: Roulette Finale by Various Authors (Coming Feb. 2023)